HONEYMOON WITH
THE BILLIONAIRE BOYS CLUB

CARA MILLER

Want my unreleased 5000-word story
Introducing the Billionaire Boys Club
and other free gifts from time to time?

Then join my mailing list at

http://www.caramillerbooks.com/inner-circle/

Subscribe now and read it now!

You can also follow me on Twitter and Facebook

Honeymoon with the Billionaire Boys Club
Copyright © 2017, Cara Miller.
All rights reserved.

An Invitation from the Billionaire Boys Club

———

Midnight with the Billionaire Boys Club

———

Dreaming with the Billionaire Boys Club

———

A Promise from the Billionaire Boys Club

———

Engaged to the Billionaire Boys Club

———

A Surprise from the Billionaire Boys Club

———

Romance with the Billionaire Boys Club

———

A Billionaire Boys Club Wedding

———

Honeymoon with the Billionaire Boys Club

Tyler kissed Kelsey as though they had been apart for years, longing for each other. It was a kiss of passion, of romance, and of pleasures to come. Kelsey, wrapped in Tyler's arms and in his love, clung to him as tightly as he held her. But slowly, reluctantly, and to Kelsey's dismay, Tyler broke away.

She knew why, of course. They were standing in front of hundreds of people, who were clapping, cheering, and taking photographs. Kelsey took a look into Tyler's sparkling brown eyes, he took her hand, and together, they headed down the aisle.

The recessional music, Handel's *The Arrival of the Queen of Sheba*, played as they walked. Tyler lifted Kelsey's hand to his lips and kissed her ring finger, and Kelsey looked at him delightedly.

We're married.

It had been such a long road, but here they were, together at last. A thousand fleeting thoughts ran through Kelsey's mind, but only one remained.

We're married, Kelsey thought. And she could think of nothing more.

Kelsey and Tyler left the aisle and were escorted back into the white tent where Kelsey had previously waited.

"Five minutes," Jeffrey said to them. And with a smile, he left them alone.

Once again, Tyler took Kelsey's face into his gentle hands, and he kissed her again. Tyler kissed her lips, her cheeks, her neck. Kelsey reached up and pulled Tyler closer. And he kissed her some more.

He stopped for a moment, just to look at her. His fingers stroked her cheek, and Kelsey felt the cool metal of his wedding ring against her warm skin. Then Tyler pulled Kelsey to himself and nuzzled her hair.

"I love you so much, Kelsey," Tyler whispered as he held her.

"I love you too, Tyler," Kelsey replied, comfortable in his strong arms. They stood together silently, as they heard the sound of their guests walking past the tent. Kelsey sighed happily, but suddenly she heard the sound of the tent door open.

"It hasn't been five minutes," Tyler said unhappily.

"It's been six," Jeffrey said unapologetically as Kelsey looked over at him. He stood by the door, with a photographer and her assistant. Tyler looked down at Kelsey and shook his head in defeat. Kelsey giggled.

After a few moments with the photographer — as she took posed photos of the couple sharing a private moment — Tyler and Kelsey left the tent. No guests were visible, but a golf cart sat next to the door of the tent. Tyler helped Kelsey into the cart, and joined her — then Jeffrey drove them a minute away, back to the grassy field. As Tyler helped Kelsey out of the golf cart, she could see that just about a hundred yards behind them, the reception was in full swing.

"Congratulations!" Lisa Olsen said brightly, giving Tyler a kiss on the cheek.

"Thanks, Mom," Tyler replied. Lisa gave a smile to Kelsey as Morgan and Jasmine walked over. It was time to take photos with the relatives that had been on the cruise ship.

Grandma Rose was the second to congratulate the couple, giving both Tyler and Kelsey big hugs. The newlywed couple took photos with her, Kelsey's parents, and Kelsey's maternal grandparents. Kelsey's father was abnormally quiet, but Kelsey's mother gave her a hug. Kelsey had barely seen her all day.

"Congratulations, honey," Kelly North said, "You look beautiful."

"Thanks for helping with the wedding," Kelsey said. Her mother nodded thoughtfully.

"Congratulations, Tyler," Kelly North said to him.

"Thanks, Kelly," Tyler replied. Kelly North gave him a small smile.

Next to Kelsey, Ryan gave a sigh.

"Here come the Norwegians," he commented.

Kelsey looked over where Ryan was looking. Four people walked towards them. One was an older blonde woman, who Kelsey assumed was Tyler's grandmother. She was accompanied by two men — slightly older than, and almost as handsome as Tyler — and a young woman.

"*Mormor*," Tyler said, greeting the older woman.

"Tyler," she replied. She glanced at Kelsey curiously. "Kelsey, I'm Lisa's mother, best wishes on your wedding day."

"Thank you," Kelsey said politely.

"Mother," Lisa Olsen said from behind Kelsey. She walked next to Kelsey and gave her mother what seemed like a very formal buss on the cheek.

"Lisa," Mrs. Olsen replied, with the same lack of enthusiasm that Kelsey had heard in Lisa Olsen's voice. The elder Mrs. Olsen surveyed her daughter. "You should cut your hair," she commented to Lisa. "You're too old to wear it so long."

Lisa was silent, but Kelsey could tell that she certainly had something that she wanted to say.

"Kelsey, these are my cousins," Tyler said, distracting Kelsey. "Niels, Kai, and Brit."

"It's nice to meet you," Kelsey said, shaking their hands.

"You look beautiful," Brit said to Kelsey.

"Thank you," Kelsey replied.

"Let's take photos," Jeffrey said to the group.

They stood, the women on the side next to Kelsey, Tyler's male cousins to his right. After several photographs were taken, the group disbanded, and Bill Simon walked up.

"Hello, Mrs. Olsen," Bill said to Lisa's mother.

"William," she said. Mrs. Olsen gave a serious look to her daughter. "Again," she added with obvious displeasure. Lisa remained silent.

"Congratulations, Kelsey," Bill Simon said.

"Thanks," Kelsey said, as she tried not to laugh.

Kelsey and Tyler took dozens of photos with various family members and close friends. Bob Perkins took a photo with Lisa and the couple, but from Kelsey's vantage point, he was much more interested in watching Morgan chat with Zach than with the photo. Finally, Kelsey and Tyler got back into the golf cart with Jeffrey, and as they drove back to the Airstream trailers, behind them their relatives began to walk the short distance to the open-air reception.

Tyler gave Kelsey a kiss on the steps of her trailer.

"I'll see you in a few minutes," Tyler said. Kelsey nodded, reached out and stroked his face, and gave him a kiss.

"OK," she said. Then she turned and walked into the trailer.

"Congratulations," Katie said to her.

"Thank you, Katie," Kelsey said, beaming.

"Mr. Smith said that you should make sure to eat something," Katie said. "He said that there won't be time to eat at the reception."

"Thank you," Kelsey repeated, taking a plate of appetizers from Katie. Kelsey knew that if Jeffrey said that there wouldn't be time, there wouldn't be any. Already they had taken hundreds, perhaps thousands of photos, and Kelsey hadn't even met most of the guests. In fact, she had no idea how they would manage to greet almost two thousand people. But Kelsey knew if there was a way, Jeffrey would have it worked out.

She ate quickly, then Katie helped her into her reception dress. It was shorter than her wedding dress, with a beaded lace cross-over bodice. Kelsey smiled as she glanced at her shiny new ring, which shone in the bright summer light.

There was a knock on the door, and Katie walked over to answer it. It was Jade, accompanied by Ray and Tania.

"Congratulations, Kelsey," Jade said happily, as she entered the room.

"Thank you," Kelsey said.

"Come on," Jade said to Ray. "There's work to do."

Kelsey sat still as Ray removed her hair from the diamond comb. It turned out that six minutes with Tyler had irreparably ruined her hairstyle, and Ray needed to work quickly to find a look that would work for her.

"Sorry," Kelsey said, as Ray pondered what to do.

"It's fine. That's what I'm paid for," he replied.

After conferring with Jeffrey, who arrived a few moments after Jade, Ray decided to let Kelsey's soft curls fall free over her bare shoulders. The comb was returned to Jeffrey, who slipped it into his breast pocket. Tania had her moment next, redoing Kelsey's makeup from scratch, as quickly as possible since Jeffrey's watchful eye was on her and the clock. Kelsey glanced in the mirror when Tania was done. Kelsey's face glowed. But Kelsey knew that it wasn't just the makeup.

"Am I done?" she asked excitedly, ready to return to her husband, who she suspected was waiting impatiently for her. Unlike Kelsey, Tyler didn't need a touch-up or costume change.

"Let's go," Jeffrey replied. Kelsey practically leapt out of her chair. It was easier now. She had changed out of her rhinestone-covered Jimmy Choos, and was now wearing a pair of beautifully-embellished flats. She and Tyler had a lot of walking around to do over the next hour, and thankfully Jeffrey had decided that she should do it in comfort.

Tyler was waiting at the foot of the stairs, and he placed his arm around Kelsey's waist and spun her around as he brought her to the ground. Kelsey giggled with joy.

"Hi, Mrs. Olsen," Tyler said, giving her a kiss on the nose.

"Mr. Olsen," Kelsey said, looking up at him.

"Let's go," Jeffrey said firmly. Tyler rolled his eyes, but they followed Jeffrey back to the golf cart.

"Did you eat?" Tyler asked Kelsey as they drove toward the reception venue.

"Of course," Kelsey said, nuzzling against him. "Did you?"

"I did," Tyler said, gently running his fingers through her hair.

"Stop it. You'll get me in trouble with the hairstylist again," Kelsey scolded.

"I don't care," Tyler replied, kissing her.

Jeffrey parked next to the white tent, and Tyler helped her out of the golf cart. Kelsey looked around in interest. She hadn't seen much of the venue before, and it was a bit of a surprise. Directly past the white tent was a long wooden path, which Kelsey realized had been built specifically for the wedding. Usually this area of Fort Worden was just grass and dirt. The path was lit for many yards, but although the path continued, the lights ended. Kelsey wondered why. But she didn't have a lot of time to wonder, because she and Tyler followed Jeffrey onto the path.

It was noisy in the comfortably warm summer air, which wasn't surprising considering the thousands of guests. Kelsey let Tyler lead her into the reception area, and they entered quietly, without fanfare. Kelsey thought she knew why. With almost two thousand guests, there was no way to personally greet everyone, but clearly Jeffrey had a plan. Kelsey and Tyler followed him as he walked through the edges of the reception area.

Kelsey looked in amazement as they quickly walked by. The reception area looked like a really large, incredibly luxurious hotel lobby. There were seating areas with leather sofas, dozens of waiters carrying trays of food and drinks, and Kelsey counted at least sixteen full bars, each with three bartenders. Their guests looked happy and comfortable.

Jeffrey led them to another grassy clearing, and to Kelsey's surprise, her Darrow classmates were waiting for her. They burst into cheers and excited applause.

"Congratulations, Kelsey!" Erica said, running up and giving Kelsey a hug.

"Thank you," Kelsey beamed. Clearly, those were likely to be the only words that Kelsey would say this evening.

"Is everyone ready?" a photographer called out. Tyler and Kelsey found themselves moved to the front of the group, and a series of photos were taken. From the corner of her eye, Kelsey saw another group of people being organized a few steps away. Their co-workers from Simon and Associates. And at that moment, Kelsey realized what Jeffrey had arranged.

Kelsey quickly discovered her theory was correct as various groups of people were organized, and Tyler and Kelsey were sent over to take photographs. After Simon and Associates, it was the Tactec executive team, then Tyler's college classmates, then Kelsey's neighbors from Port Townsend. Group after group received greetings, then photographs were taken, then Kelsey and Tyler were moved to the next group. Tyler hugged Sophia when the Law Review group took their photo, Kelsey was pleased to meet Tyler's friends from high school, and Kelsey got a special greeting from a former Portland State classmate.

"Congratulations, Kelsey," said a well-dressed Dylan, giving her a kiss on the cheek. A beaming Ian looked on.

Finally, after taking pictures with the two former Presidents and their families, surrounded by the Secret Service, they seemed to have finished with the groups. Kelsey had no idea how everyone had been organized so quickly, although she could see that there were numerous assistants running around. She and Tyler had even taken photos with what Kelsey assumed was the billionaire group, because in addition to Lisa and Bob being there, she had recognized at least six of the people from their covers on various business magazines.

Kelsey lifted the hem of her dress gently with her free hand as Tyler held her other hand and guided her through the mass of guests. They were once again following Jeffrey, who now held a large Tactec tablet, and they were all now followed by Jade, still in her bridesmaid dress. Kelsey had to admit that the idea had been a brilliant one. Few people were likely to remember if Jade had been in the wedding, and her dress let her blend in.

Kelsey caught a glimpse of Jeffrey's tablet, which featured what seemed to be a curving road, with a number of moving stars visible along the path. One of the stars suddenly became larger on the tablet, and Jeffrey brought them to a stop.

"Mr. Beckindale, may I present Tyler and Kelsey Olsen?" Jeffrey said to the older man, who was sipping a drink.

"Congratulations," Mr. Beckindale said, shaking Tyler's hand. Kelsey smiled politely as she surveyed the man. They had taken a group photo with him earlier.

Edwin Beckindale was the third richest man in the country this year, according to the media.

"It's nice to finally meet you," Tyler said.

"It's surprising our paths haven't crossed earlier. I've known your mother for a decade. This is my wife, Helena."

"Hello," Helena Beckindale said as she stepped next to her husband, and Kelsey and Tyler made their greetings. Helena Beckindale looked at least twenty years younger than her husband.

After a few moments of small talk, Tyler and Kelsey said their goodbyes and walked on, following Jeffrey. As they walked, Kelsey noticed that Jeffrey tapped the large star, which then disappeared from the tablet, and a second star suddenly became larger and brighter. And they stopped for another introduction.

It took a few more introductions before Kelsey realized what was going on. She knew that every guest was wearing a locator bracelet for security reasons. And because of the sheer number of guests, they had decided not to have a receiving line, which would have taken hours to get through. That was the reason for the group photographs. But there were still guests that it would be important to greet in person.

Kelsey looked at the tablet in Jeffrey's hand. Although it wouldn't be obvious to others, he was leading them on a computer-generated road lined with the most important guests. As the guests moved, so did their stars, and the computer gently adjusted the road. As they got closer, the stars enlarged to alert Jeffrey that they were in range to say hello to a VIP guest. Once the greeting was done, a simple tap of the screen removed the guest from the list.

Kelsey marveled at the technology. She was surprised that she hadn't noticed photographs of their targets on the tablet, but she supposed that Jeffrey knew who most of them were. They would be mostly billionaires, after all.

One of the VIP guests that Kelsey wasn't surprised to meet was Chris's ex-girlfriend Liz. Tyler beamed as he introduced her to Kelsey.

"Finally," Liz said to Kelsey, giving her a big hug.

Kelsey looked at Liz as the older woman gave Tyler a hug. When Tyler had mentioned that Liz was an art professor, Kelsey had a vision of what she must look like firmly in mind. Gray streaks in her hair, a little rumpled, with granny glasses. But obviously, Kelsey hadn't seen an art professor in a while. Liz was tall, with glossy brown hair, and radiated bohemian chic. She wore a beaded necklace around her neck, and her arm was covered in silver bangles.

"You two look so happy," Liz said.

"We'll be happier when this is over," Tyler commented.

"Oh, Tyler," Liz scolded. "So, Kelsey, do you like your engagement ring?"

"I love it," Kelsey enthused.

"I told you," Tyler said to Liz.

"Maybe," Liz said to him. "You're just like Chris. Mr. Know-it-all."

"Have you managed to avoid him?" Tyler asked.

"I have," Liz said.

"Is something going on that I need to know about?" Tyler asked in concern.

Liz shook her glossy hair. "We ran into each other in Soho, and it was a little tense. I wanted to have fun this weekend, particularly since I've never been on a cruise before. It was so nice that your mother arranged that for us."

"Have you met Lisa?" Tyler asked Liz, but smiled at Kelsey.

"I did, Tyler," Liz said. "Actually, I was a little nervous, but she was very gracious. She said that I was your East Coast mom. I wasn't expecting that at all. She's quite charming."

"Charming," Tyler said.

"I'm serious. I thought she was really nice. Having said that, I understand why your father couldn't manage to stay married to her."

"What's your theory?" Tyler asked.

"I get the sense that your mother was too intense for him. Chris likes to spend the weekend, hanging out, doing chores, watching the game. I can't imagine Lisa Olsen doing that with him."

"That's an interesting theory," Tyler said.

"You have a different one, Ty?" Liz asked.

"No," Tyler hedged. "That seems like a good one," he said noncommittally.

Liz gave Tyler a look, but she didn't press the point.

"So when are you and Kelsey coming back to the East Coast?"

"When we can," Tyler said. "We're both working now, so it might be a while."

"Kelsey, I understand that you like working for Tyler's former boss."

"Bill's great," Kelsey said.

"Kelsey likes everyone," Tyler commented.

Liz laughed. "Perhaps you can teach that skill to Tyler," she said to Kelsey.

"I like lots of people," Tyler said in his defense. "Just not Chris."

"Try to get along with him. He means well."

"I could say the same to you."

"I'm in a different kind of relationship with your father," Liz pointed out. "You don't constantly have to deal with the ghost of his ex-wife."

Tyler shrugged. "I"m not sure that's true."

Liz smiled at him. "My guess is that after today's events, Chris will mellow out about Lisa."

"You think so?" Tyler said curiously.

Liz nodded. "I think that really upset him, Tyler. He managed to get you back, but I think a part of him couldn't believe that he walked away from half of Tactec."

"Maybe," Tyler said. "So what does that mean for you?"

"For me?" Liz asked curiously.

"Will you forgive Chris if he moves on from being angry with Lisa?"

Liz frowned, and her perfect forehead wrinkled just a little.

"We'll see. Like I said, I'm in a different kind of relationship with him."

After chatting with Liz, and after meeting a few more guests, they paused briefly and a smiling assistant, dressed in a pretty navy-blue dress, presented them with cold drinks and appetizers to enjoy.

"Eat," Jeffrey ordered. "You won't have another chance for at least a half-hour."

Kelsey and Tyler didn't have to be told twice. Their wedding day had been overwhelming, and they hadn't made it to dinner yet.

Tyler offered Kelsey a mini-tourtiere tart, and she ate it from his fingers. His brown eyes sparkled, and although Kelsey was tired, she felt a surge of strength from the loving look he gave her. He kissed her hand, right next to her glowing wedding band, and Kelsey felt his heat. Tyler leaned over and kissed her cheek. He whispered in her ear,

"A few more hours, Mrs. Olsen." Then he kissed her once again.

Kelsey was exhausted. She and Tyler were back in the white tent, waiting as their guests were being seated for dinner. Tyler's lawyer had come into the tent a few minutes earlier with Zach, Morgan, and Pastor Nelson, and had the couple sign a bunch of paperwork, including their marriage license. Kelsey sat on Tyler's lap and rested her head against his.

"How are you doing, Mrs. Olsen?" Tyler asked. His arms were around her waist, and his eyes were closed.

"Who knew weddings were such hard work?" Kelsey asked.

"We'll be able to sit and regain our strength soon," Tyler commented. "I hope," he added.

A few minutes later, Kelsey and Tyler were once again following Jeffrey along the wooden path. As they passed the now-empty reception area, Kelsey realized how the path worked. Ahead of them, the path lights were now lit, far beyond the reception area, but not all the way to the end of the path. The lights were a guide for the guests. They were lit only as far as the next destination, and that was where Kelsey and Tyler were walking to now. They paused briefly on the path as they got within sight of dozens of circular dining tables, then they began walking again. Kelsey heard through the summer air,

"Let's give a warm welcome to Mr. and Mrs. Tyler Olsen!"

As the crowd applauded, they entered the table area. Hands clasped together, Kelsey and Tyler followed Jeffrey's directions, and walked off the wooden path, onto an enormous wooden floor, which had been laid down over the ground. No one's fabulous shoes would need to touch the grass at this wedding. Although Kelsey knew it was temporary, and probably necessary, the flooring that was absolutely everywhere made the outdoor wedding seem a little less outdoorsy. But Kelsey knew it was a concession to her guests, who were dressed in their finery.

Kelsey and Tyler walked up to a stage at the front, where there was a table with two place settings, and next to it, a small podium. Clearly the bride and groom would be the stars of this particular show. Kelsey felt a tiny bit self-conscious as she sat in her seat, but of course, she was the bride, and all eyes would be on her tonight, whether she was comfortable or not. Tyler sat next to her, and they listened as the master of ceremonies, Holden Johnson, talked to the crowd. Kelsey watched him in awe. She was surprised that he had managed to take time away from his top-rated television show to be the master of ceremonies at her wedding.

Mr. Johnson introduced both sets of parents, the bridesmaids, and the groomsmen as Kelsey looked out onto the audience. It was such a large number of people.

"And now," Holden Johnson said, "I'd like to invite the bride and groom to have their first dance." Tyler stood, smiled at Kelsey, and held out his hand. She smiled back, took his hand, and let him lead her off the stage and down to the front, where a large space was available for them to dance.

The jazz band that sat near the front began to play the classic song, *At Last,* and as Tyler took Kelsey into his arms, the singer began to sing the lyrics. Kelsey tried to remember all of the steps that it had taken her weeks to learn, and she concentrated as she swayed in Tyler's strong, secure arms. Finally, to Kelsey's relief, the song concluded, and as the audience applauded appreciatively, Tyler led Kelsey back to her seat.

Tyler remained standing, because he had a speech to give. As Kelsey sat comfortably and had a sip of water, she was very happy to be the bride. Although she knew that Tyler wouldn't mind, the last thing that she wanted to do today was to give a speech in front of thousands of guests. It was bad enough that she had needed to dance in front of them.

After being introduced by the master of ceremonies, Tyler confidently looked out into the audience, and began.

"Ladies and gentlemen, the first person I would like to thank tonight is my new father-in-law, Daniel North. Without question, I would not be standing here tonight if it were not for him and for my lovely mother-in-law, Kelly. They have welcomed me into their home and into their lives, stood by us through some trying situations, and been invaluable to me. I will always be grateful to you, Dan and Kelly.

"I would also like to thank my parents, Lisa Olsen and Christopher Davis. I love and care for both of you deeply, and I'm happy that both of you are here to share in our special day. I look forward to all of us celebrating together in the future as Kelsey and I grow as a couple.

"Next, I would like to thank Kelsey's three wonderful bridesmaids, Morgan Hill, Jasmine Brennan, and Jessica Perkins. I know how much Kelsey relies on your friendship and I'm thankful that each of you could be here to share this moment with us.

"As for my best man, Zachary Payne, you already know that if it were not for you, I might have never asked Kelsey out in the first place. And I owe a debt of gratitude to both Brandon Kinnon and Ryan Perkins as well. I would not be the man I am today without your friendship.

"The events of this wedding weekend reflect the hard work of hundreds of people, but I would be remiss if I did not single out my longtime assistant, Jeffrey Smith. Jeffrey has given up his nights, weekends, and I imagine much of his sleep over the past four months, in order to put this wedding together, and my family and I give him our greatest thanks.

"Finally," Tyler said, and he looked over at Kelsey, "I want to thank my beautiful wife, Kelsey for making me the luckiest man in the world today. You mean everything to me, and I look forward to a lifetime of being your husband."

Kelsey smiled at Tyler. He smiled back and turned back to the audience.

"Thanks to all of you for coming and being with us here tonight. It means everything to us that you are here. Please join me in a toast to my bride, Kelsey."

Tyler raised his glass, along with the audience, and drank to Kelsey. Then Tyler walked over, gave Kelsey a gentle kiss and sat next to her. Kelsey took his hand, and leaned her head on his shoulder for a second.

"Thank you," she said.

"Thank you for marrying me," Tyler said, kissing her again.

"That was a wonderful speech," Kelsey commented. Tyler had managed to give a speech that hit all of the correct notes, acknowledging the turmoil of their journey to this day without dwelling on it. Kelsey felt that he had been particularly gracious to her mother, and to his own. He had needed to write the speech thoughtfully, as everyone who sat in the audience would know about the proxy fight with Tactec. Tyler had married the woman who had represented him in his lawsuit against his mother's company, after all.

"Thanks," Tyler said dismissively "Jeffrey wrote it." Kelsey looked at him in surprise.

"I just want to get this over with," Tyler said.

Kelsey stroked his arm and gave him a loving look. Kelsey had to agree with Tyler's sentiment. Their families and guests seemed to be having a nice time, judging from the happy laughter and many hugs Kelsey had seen. But the bridal couple had been on what could only be called a conveyor belt between one photo opportunity after another. Kelsey was happy to have this quiet moment, and she leaned on Tyler again.

It wasn't that Kelsey wasn't grateful. Jeffrey's meticulous work was everywhere. Even now, as Kelsey looked into the audience, she could see that the majority of women in the crowd were wrapped in navy-blue pashminas, which Kelsey knew to be decorated with the entwined K and T logo that symbolized the wedding. Kelsey had also noticed that Helena Beckindale wasn't carrying a designer evening bag tonight, but instead she held a mini canvas bag with the same logo and an adorable nautical motif.

As the wind blew gently through the dinner tables, so did the sound of excited children, the sons and daughters of their guests — playing on a custom-built playground steps away, and watched over by professionally-trained nannies. This little detail she knew from Jess, who had commented that it was too bad that the unborn twins weren't able to play on the hand-crafted wooden ship.

As Kelsey sat and looked out into the dozens of tables laden with flowers and watched her guests take photos with their brand new Tactec tablets, she marvelled at the fact that this was her wedding. But there was a little part of her that was sorry that she was missing the many details that Jeffrey had worked so hard on.

The master of ceremonies took command again, and introduced Kelsey's father, who rose and walked up to the podium.

Kelsey leaned against Tyler and squeezed his hand as her father unfolded a piece of paper and put on his reading glasses. She wasn't nervous. She was curious. The fathers had been asked to speak not of their own children, but of their children's new spouses.

Kelsey believed that it had been a wise decision. Chris and Tyler still were struggling with their relationship, and Kelsey wasn't confident that Chris would have a lot of nice things to say about his son at this moment. Since Chris still didn't know Kelsey that well, she supposed that he would find a few pleasantries to speak about. As for her own father, Kelsey thought she knew what Dan North thought of Tyler, but she wondered what else he might have to say.

Dan North looked a little unnerved as he looked out onto the massive crowd, and Kelsey wasn't surprised. He wasn't used to public speaking, and certainly had never spoken to such a large crowd. He cleared his throat and began.

"Once my precious little girl became a teenager, I thought I knew the kind of guy that Kelsey would bring home. A rebel. A guy with bunch of tattoos and a lot of attitude. A boy who wasn't afraid to stand up to my outspoken, headstrong daughter. So I had my plan all ready.

"I spoke to my friend Walt, who has four daughters of his own, and who understood my fears perfectly. We made a pact between us. One for all and all for one. Any unsuitable guy gets near any of our daughters, and we throw him out together."

That explains Eric, Kelsey thought.

"I expected drama and pleading on that day, but I would be steadfast, because obviously, no guy like that would be good enough for my daughter. And once Kelsey left for school, I just figured I'd wait to see the jerk that Kelsey would bring home, and be ready to throw him off the property. He'd be easy to spot. He would be the one I couldn't stand.

"So I thought nothing at all when Tyler walked through the door of our house. A smart, interesting young man who's pleasant to talk to? A law school classmate? Of course he's not the kind of guy my daughter would go for, I said confidently to myself. So I resumed my post and listened for a motorcycle outside my door, ridden by some lunkhead ready to try to steal my only daughter away.

"In the meantime, the man who's actually going to steal my daughter away is in my shed, helping me with a woodworking project.

"Tyler asked me for Kelsey's hand in marriage, and I said yes. But a part of me didn't believe it. Kelsey said yes to Tyler, and I still wasn't convinced. My wife started dragging in bridal magazines, and took over a room with wedding favors, but I'm still looking outside, sure that Kelsey's going to ride up on the back of some idiot's Harley, and he's going to tell me that they're in love.

"But now here we are.

"I've been trying to think why I was so wrong. It wasn't because I underestimated my daughter. Kelsey's a beautiful, intelligent young woman. It wasn't because I thought she couldn't pick a good man.

"It was because I wasn't sure that a good man would see how he could fit in the life of a woman as independent as Kelsey. I know that there's no shortage of overconfident idiots. But what good man would be confident enough in his own self to see my daughter and realize what a rare find she was?

"It seems as though Tyler Olsen is that good man.

"In a month or two, I'll feel OK about handing my daughter over to Tyler at the altar. In a year or so, I'll start remembering how when Tyler walked into our house one holiday weekend, that I said to my mother that Tyler Olsen was exactly the kind of warm, kind person that I wished that Kelsey would fall in love with. And a few years after that, I'll realize just how unbelievably lucky that I am that someone as special as Tyler came into Kelsey's life.

"But it's tonight. And I have to apologize, but I'm still in shock because the tiny baby that I brought home from the hospital yesterday is now a married woman. So let's toast Kelsey and Tyler, because I think that I need a drink."

Kelsey burst out laughing, along with Tyler and much of the audience. Dan North picked up his glass, and said,

"Congratulations." And he drained his glass.

As the audience laughed and applauded, Dan North walked over to Kelsey and she stood and gave him a long hug. Tyler stood and shook his hand. Then Kelsey's father walked back over to his wife, who handed him her handkerchief.

"That was cute," Kelsey giggled as she gave the smiling Tyler a cuddle. Christopher Davis stood up next and took his place at the front of the room.

"Next," said the M.C., "we'll hear from the groom's father, Chris Davis."

Chris gave Kelsey a glance, then began.

"When I was first asked to speak about Kelsey, I considered declining in favor of Tyler's mother, Lisa. Unfortunately, I haven't spent a lot of time with Kelsey. And the time that I have spent has been largely monopolized by my son and me talking about our own concerns over dinners together.

"But when I mentioned this, I was told that the same was true of Lisa and Kelsey. They've shared a few family dinners and little more.

"So then my next thought was why, as Tyler's father, was I completely unconcerned about my son marrying Kelsey?

"This bothered me for a few days. I know that Tyler has a good head on his shoulders, and is quite capable of choosing his own wife, but didn't I have the responsibility to judge Kelsey myself, and let Tyler know if I had any issues with his bride?

"Tyler and I spent the year before he met Kelsey together, a wonderful year. I learned a lot about the young man that he's grown up to be. But as any father does, I saw flaws in my son. A few rough edges that needed to be fixed.

"Time went on, and Tyler returned to the West Coast. I called, I Skyped, I meddled. That's what fathers do. And Tyler did what sons do. He ignored me.

"A while later, I came out to Seattle to have dinner with Tyler. He asked if he could bring along a classmate. Kelsey North. I agreed, but I made it clear to Tyler that I was coming out to talk business, father to son. I wouldn't let his classmate get in my way.

"Tyler agreed, and I was introduced to Kelsey. I could stop here and say all of the things you would expect me to say about her. How gracious and intelligent she is. The care and love that she shows to my son. However, the moment that I met her, I was on a mission. To correct my son. So at first, I barely noticed she was there. That says nothing about Kelsey, everything about me.

"Kelsey didn't speak much during that dinner, or the ones that Tyler and I have had with her since. To be honest, Tyler and I have a tendency to take up all of the space for conversation. But later I realized something. Kelsey didn't have to speak to me to make her presence known. Because she had already changed Tyler.

"This is actually fascinating to me. I've always been one of those men who think that an individual controls their destiny. That relationships are nice, but not completely necessary. That a man can have a goal, strike out on his own, and create an empire.

"But now, I'm starting to rethink that view. Kelsey makes Tyler better. He's a different person than the young man who lived with me just a few years ago. He's more thoughtful, more self-aware. And I should have realized that the moment that Kelsey sat down at the table on the night that I met her. Without a word, she changed the dynamic between me and my son.

"It is difficult to be so far away from your child, just at the moment when you think that you need to be there to give them a good foundation on their road to being a successful adult. But I am grateful to Tyler's mother for raising him with a lot of love, and to Kelsey, who has been an amazing influence on Tyler already, and who is going to be a wonderful wife. I look forward to more family dinners where I can spend time with the extraordinary woman who loves, and is loved by, my extraordinary son."

Chris raised his glass and toasted the couple,

"To Kelsey and Tyler."

The audience raised their glasses and drank, then broke out into applause as Chris walked over to Tyler and Kelsey, hugged them both, then walked off stage. Kelsey watched as he walked to his seat. He was sitting with the Parker side of the family. Kelsey thought it was a wise choice on Jeffrey's part.

"Let's enjoy our dinner with the happy couple for a few moments. Then, we will hear from the maid of honor and the best man," said the Master of Ceremonies.

The dinnertime jazz music began again. A server brought their dinners to them. Kelsey had ordered the vegan African dinner. According to Jeffrey, over half the guests had ordered the African-themed dinner. Out of curiosity, Kelsey supposed. She was very pleased to see the meal that was placed in front of her. It was Ethiopian — numerous vegetable dishes plated on top of injera bread. Tyler, who had ordered the Northwestern cuisine meal, had salmon.

"What did you think of Chris's speech?" she asked.

Tyler looked thoughtful for a moment. "I think I have to ponder that one for a while. I'm glad he likes you, though," he concluded.

Kelsey nodded, and offered Tyler a piece of her injera bread, which he ate happily. She had to agree, Chris's speech was quite interesting on a lot of levels. She was surprised, to start, that Chris had praised Lisa.

"So do you know what Morgan is going to say?" Tyler asked Kelsey.

"No, she hasn't told me anything," Kelsey replied, after swallowing a portion of her own dinner. "What about Zach?"

"Not a word," Tyler said. He shrugged. "Are you having a good night?"

"With you, I am," Kelsey replied.

Tyler gave her a kiss. "I look forward to making it better," he said seductively. Kelsey felt herself blush.

Time elapsed, and Kelsey and Tyler made the most of it by finishing their dinners. The speeches were being filmed, and it felt awkward to eat while someone was praising you a few steps away. The MC returned to the front and spoke to the crowd.

"Now I'm pleased to present the maid of honor, Morgan Hill, and the best man, Zachary Payne."

There was polite applause as both Morgan and Zach got up on stage together.

"Why are they going up together?" Kelsey whispered to Tyler.

"I'm not sure I want to know," Tyler said apprehensively.

"Hello, everyone," Morgan said brightly. Kelsey noted how poised she was. "Zach and I were asked to give speeches tonight."

"However," Zach said into the microphone, "Morgan and I thought that we should do something just a little different this evening."

"Oh, no," Kelsey said under her breath. She glanced at Tyler, who looked displeased.

"It's tradition," Zach went on, "that the best man and the maid of honor give speeches at this point in the evening. And it's also tradition that one of two things happen. Either they lie, and say how perfect the bride and groom are, or they tell the truth and that ends their friendships. Morgan and I have known Kelsey and Tyler too long not to be honest with you, but we also want to stay friends with them."

"So," Morgan said happily, "We decided to let someone else take on our traditional roles, and we asked who would give you the honest truth, without damaging their relationships with the bride and groom. So Zach and I asked ourselves, who is the last person on earth that Tyler would want to toast him, and who is the last person that Kelsey would choose? And we asked those people to give the speeches instead."

Tyler and Kelsey looked at each other in shock. Kelsey's mind raced. Who would Morgan pick for her? Who would Zach pick for Tyler?

Kelsey didn't have to wait for long to answer the second question, as the glamorous Mrs. Kim Lee stood and walked towards the front. Tyler glared at Zach, who gave him a big grin back.

"I would like to welcome my replacement for the evening, Mrs. Kimberly Lee," Zach said. Kim, who had arrived at the front, gave Zachary a peck on the cheek, flipped her long black hair over her shoulder, and looked out into the audience without a glance at Tyler.

"Tyler Davis Olsen is no fun," Kim declared, and there were some chuckles around the audience. Tyler, on the other hand, from the look on his face, clearly wasn't amused.

"I met Tyler years ago, through our mutual friend Ryan. Tyler's about five minutes older than Ryan, but he acts like Ryan's elder brother. And mine too. On a dull weekend, Ryan and I would come up with interesting things to do, and there would always be Tyler, ready to kill the fun."

Kelsey glanced over at her new husband, who was frowning. Kim went on.

"This went on for a long time. I'd always ask Ryan, why are you asking Tyler's opinion, because you know he's going to just say no to anything we want to do. And Ryan would say, Kimmy, you should listen to Tyler more, because he knows the right thing to do."

Kim flipped her hair dramatically.

"But I just thought Tyler was boring," she stated flatly, And the audience laughed at her delivery.

"It took me a long time to realize that Tyler's not saying no because he doesn't like fun. He's saying no because he doesn't want you to get hurt," Kim said, and her voice became thoughtful, almost melancholy. "Tyler's the kind of guy who stops you from running the stop sign, because he's spotted the police car hiding behind it. I realized much too late, that if I had listened to Tyler, that I could have saved myself a lot of heartache. Lucky for me, I finally decided to take his advice."

Kim glanced over her shoulder and looked at Tyler, who was finally smiling.

"One thing that I know is that if Tyler is willing to fight to protect me from my own stupidity, he's certainly going to fight to protect the woman that he loves. Although it took me years to appreciate Tyler's qualities, it's clear that Kelsey saw them right away. Tyler once told me that he liked smart girls, and I think that it is pretty obvious that Kelsey's one of the smartest in the room, because she picked Tyler Olsen to marry."

Kim picked up her glass, and turned toward the couple.

"I wish the both of you the best of luck. Kelsey, you couldn't have picked a better man to marry."

Kelsey beamed as Kim said,

"To Kelsey and Tyler."

The audience drank to Kim's toast, and Zachary escorted Kim off stage as the audience applauded her.

Kelsey's nerves began as Morgan returned to the microphone and spoke.

"Without further ado, my replacement, Mr. Jace Jefferson."

Kelsey's jaw dropped as Jace walked to the stage. Morgan — wisely, Kelsey supposed — did not look over at the bridal couple, but instead greeted Jace with a fist bump, and left the stage.

Jace began to speak.

"Kelsey North has been a thorn in my side every since she convinced my baby sister that they should paint my bedroom wall pink because it 'needed a little color'."

Kelsey stifled a giggle. Jace had lived with a neon-pink splotch on his bedroom wall for months, until Papa Jefferson had taken pity on him and agreed to repaint the room.

"Kelsey doesn't get into trouble. She is trouble. So when she brought this guy, Tyler Olsen home, I didn't expect much. In fact, when I met him, I assumed he was insane. He would have to be to put up with Kelsey North."

"But I came back a few months later, and Tyler Olsen was also back again. And I spoke to him, and realized that he wasn't crazy at all. And this was really puzzling to me. Here's this pretty normal guy, and he's head over heels in love with Kelsey."

"And I asked myself, what would anyone see in her?"

Kelsey felt herself frown, but she sat silently.

Jace paused for a moment, then began to speak again.

"I know that Kelsey loves her family and is completely loyal to her friends, but I also realized that many of the things that drive me crazy about Kelsey are the qualities that you should want in a wife. The most important quality is that no matter what, more than anything, Kelsey never, ever quits.

"No matter what the odds, Kelsey will never give up. And in a world where there is so much pressure to give in, to compromise your principles and to let others determine where your life should go, everyone should be lucky enough to have someone like Kelsey. Someone to remind you that you only fail when you stop trying.

"In a cage match between Kelsey and a bear, I'd put my money on Kelsey. And I've been to a lot of weddings lately, and I'm putting my money on this one. When you have two people this devoted to each other, so completely in love, you can't help but marvel at what brought them together, and know that nothing can tear them apart. Let's raise a glass to Mr. and Mrs. Tyler Olsen."

Jace raised his glass with the audience, then drank with them. Jace turned to Kelsey, gave her a wink, then walked off stage as the audience applauded.

Tyler gave Kelsey's forehead a kiss.

"We survived, he noted, as the jazz band began to play again. Kelsey saw Jeffrey approach the stage, and sighed to herself. It was a good thing that she had finished dinner. He walked over to the couple.

"A few of your guests would like to take photos with you before you change, Kelsey," Jeffrey said to her. Tyler squeezed her hand, and they both rose. Break time was officially over.

A half-hour later, Kelsey was escorted back to her dressing trailer by Jade. To her surprise, Ryan and Jess were there, curled up sleepily on the sofa.

"Are you OK?" Kelsey asked Jessica, in concern.

"I thought I'd better take a nap after dinner," Jessica yawned. She looked at Ryan and stroked his face gently. "Get out," she commanded.

Ryan looked at her, puzzled.

"Kelsey needs to change," Jessica explained.

"She doesn't have anything I haven't seen before," Ryan commented as he stood up.

"Get out, Ryan," Kelsey snapped. Ryan laughed, but left the trailer.

Jessica sat up on the sofa. "How's it going?" she asked. "How's married life?"

Kelsey laughed. "If I had more than three seconds to talk to Tyler, I might be able to tell you."

"Weddings are like that, Kels," Jessica said. "I don't remember anything from our wedding. I have to look at the pictures to figure out who was there, besides you, me, and Ryan."

"I understand now," Kelsey said, as she unzipped the back of her dress. "It's crazy out there."

Jessica stood up slowly from the sofa. "Can I help with anything?" she asked as Kelsey stepped out of her dress.

"It's OK," Kelsey said, as she reached for the third dress of the night and put it on. Kelsey smiled as she looked in the mirror on the wall of the trailer. The designer had turned Grandma's 70's-style wedding dress nightmare into a beautiful dream. Kelsey adjusted the dress around her waist, as Tania walked in and began gathering her supplies to retouch Kelsey's makeup.

Jessica looked at her. "You look so happy, Mrs. Olsen," she commented as she zipped up Kelsey's dress.

Kelsey beamed. "I never thought this day would come," she admitted. There had been so many ups and downs in their path to the altar, Kelsey didn't want to think of them all. But now she was Mrs. Tyler Olsen, and none of that mattered anymore.

A few minutes later, Kelsey carefully stepped out of the trailer, and Tyler stood at the foot of the stairs. He reached out his hand and helped her down the stairs.

"Wow," he said.

"It's amazing what they did with Grandma's dress," Kelsey said, turning one way, then the other, letting the cream-colored silk graze her legs.

Tyler shook his head. "I'm not looking at the dress," he said.

"No?" Kelsey teased.

"No," Tyler said definitively. He stroked her arm, leaned down, and kissed her. Kelsey blushed at the look he gave her. "I'm looking at you."

Kelsey turned her head shyly, and Tyler took her hand into his own.

Ryan walked up. "Is Jess still there?" he asked.

Kelsey looked at him and nodded yes. "I think she's trying not to fall asleep," Kelsey said.

"You can go home," Tyler said to Ryan. "I think you guys are done for the night. It's not like Jess wants to catch the bouquet."

"We'll stick around. Just let Jeffrey know that we're napping in the trailer," Ryan said.

"He can wake you up for cake," Tyler said, as he and Kelsey began walking toward the golf cart.

Jeffrey drove Tyler and Kelsey past the empty reception area, where all that remained were the sofas and empty bars. They passed by the slowly-emptying dining area, where a handful of guests were sitting around talking, while servers cleaned up around them. Finally, they drove by what seemed to be the end of the path, and parked behind a second, smaller stage. Kelsey could hear but not see the venue where their guests were, because her view was blocked by the stage. Tyler helped her carefully out of the car. She was wearing heels again, although she knew, because Jeffrey had told her, that Morgan had a pair of flat jeweled sandals waiting for Kelsey to change into after the father/daughter dance. Tyler guided her over the first grass Kelsey had seen in a while, and to the flooring, which was nestled next to the stage.

The sun had been gently setting as the evening had gone on, and had made a rosy glow. But now it was almost gone, and Kelsey saw beautiful strings of white lights hanging from flower-covered poles.

Tyler and Kelsey walked to the empty dance floor directly below the stage, and as they were spotted by the guests, the Master of Ceremonies introduced them again. Then he said,

"Can I please welcome Mr. Daniel North to the dance floor?"

And Kelsey smiled as her father walked up to the couple. Tyler graciously relinquished Kelsey's hand and left the dance floor, leaving her in the arms of her father.

"Are you crying?" Kelsey asked in surprise, as the song *Because You Loved Me* began, and her father gently swept her around the dance floor.

"Of course not," Daniel North said, but Kelsey could clearly see tears in his eyes.

"Daddy, I'll be fine," Kelsey said. From the corner of her eye, she could see Tyler speaking to his own mother. They would join Kelsey and her father on the dance floor in a moment.

Dan North nodded, but was silent.

"Your speech was really good," Kelsey said, in an attempt to distract him.

"I meant every word. It didn't hit me that you were getting married until about a month ago."

"Why did you think that Tyler asked you for my hand in marriage then?" Kelsey teased.

Dan North shrugged. He looked at Kelsey, and kissed her forehead.

"I can't believe you're married," he said in disbelief.

After Tyler and Lisa joined them, and the song ended, the dance floor opened to the other guests, and Tyler escorted Kelsey off the dance floor to look for Morgan. The rest of Kelsey's dances would be in more comfortable shoes.

She looked around, but with all of the guests, it was difficult to spot Morgan.

"There she is," Tyler said. Kelsey looked where he was looking. Morgan was sitting at one of the small, more intimate tables that surrounded the dance floor. But she wasn't sitting alone.

Next to her, Bob Perkins was sitting in a chair next to her, talking. Tyler and Kelsey watched as Bob reached out and took Morgan's hand into his own.

"Let's get your shoes," Tyler commented, gently pulling Kelsey toward Morgan. Morgan looked up as they approached. She withdrew her hand from Bob's and reached under the table, pulling out a cloth bag.

"Here you are," Morgan said.

"Thanks," Kelsey replied, sitting down in the empty chair next to Morgan, and taking the bag.

"The party's going well," Bob commented to Tyler.

"Lisa paid enough for it," Tyler replied.

Bob laughed. "You're very cynical, Mr. Olsen," Bob commented.

"Maybe," Tyler conceded.

"You'll have Kelsey to yourself soon enough. Let her family enjoy some time with her," Bob commented.

"Bob," Morgan scolded as Kelsey changed shoes. Kelsey wiggled her painted toes before putting on the new shoes. She put the red-soled Christian Louboutin shoes into the cloth bag, and handed the bag back to Morgan. Her new shoes were Christian Louboutin as well, but they were rhinestone flats instead of heels. As always, Kelsey put the expense of what she was wearing out of her mind.

"Are you having fun, babe?" Morgan asked.

"It's really busy," Kelsey admitted.

"It's about to get busier," Tyler commented. Kelsey looked up. Jeffrey was briskly walking towards them. "It was nice talking to you," Tyler said wryly.

Bob laughed. "We'll see you later," he said.

"Don't forget to throw the bouquet to Anna," Morgan said, as Kelsey stood.

"Not you?" Bob asked. Morgan gave him a look.

"I'm not dating anyone, Mr. Perkins. But you knew that," Morgan replied.

"Really?" Bob said, as if he was hearing it for the first time. "A pretty girl like you?"

"I didn't say I haven't been asked," Morgan replied sassily. Bob looked at her darkly, but before he could reply, Jeffrey arrived at the table.

"Kelsey, Hannah's family is leaving, and she wanted to say goodbye," Jeffrey reported.

"OK, we'll get going," Kelsey said. She glanced at Morgan, who was twirling her hair. Something was clearly going on underneath Morgan's banter with Bob, but Kelsey had no time to think about it as she and Tyler walked away from the table.

"What was that about?" Tyler asked Kelsey.

"No idea," Kelsey said. Jeffrey, Tactec tablet in hand, expertly guided them through the hundreds of small tables where guests were having conversations, enjoying drinks, and scrolling through wedding photos. The tablets that every guest had received as a gift included a wedding app that allowed everyone to upload and share the pictures they took during the evening. People could look through the photos and save their favorites, and the very best were being displayed behind the DJ, who was playing some of Kelsey's favorite songs. Every so often the couple was stopped by a guest to take a photo, or to have a quick chat, so it took a while to get to Hannah.

"Kelsey!" Hannah said happily as they arrived. Lily looked at Kelsey sleepily. She was wrapped in a navy pashmina. Riley yawned. Hannah gave Kelsey a hug.

"You aren't driving back to Gig Harbor tonight?" Kelsey asked in concern.

Hannah shook her head no. "We'll stay at the hotel again. Aunt Kelly is going to have brunch at her house tomorrow. Will you and Tyler be there?"

Kelsey glanced at Tyler.

"No," Kelsey said. She still didn't know where they were going for their honeymoon, but she knew for a fact that Tyler would not be planning on joining his in-laws for brunch the day after his wedding.

Kelsey leaned down and gave both children hugs and kisses.

"Thank you for being in my wedding," she said to them.

"It was fun," Riley said. "I liked the ship."

"Riley's going to be talking about that ship for months," Hannah said. "They had a lot of fun, but I think we'd better leave before dessert. All of that sugar will make them hyper, and I won't be able to get them to go to sleep."

"OK," Kelsey giggled. "It was good seeing you."

"Don't be a stranger. Gig Harbor isn't that far from Seattle. Tyler, welcome to the crazy Parker family."

Tyler grinned. "Thanks, Hannah," he said. Hannah took her sleepy children's hands, and she headed away from the couple.

Before Jeffrey could speak, Tyler said, "Two minutes."

"Two," Jeffrey conceded, and he walked off, leaving Tyler and Kelsey alone. Tyler and Kelsey sat at an empty table, and Tyler kissed Kelsey on the lips.

"We should go," Tyler said. "Now."

"Tyler, you know we can't. We haven't even cut the cake," Kelsey replied with a smile. "You can't sneak out of your own wedding reception."

"I knew we should have eloped," Tyler said, leaning over and kissing her again.

Too quickly, Jeffrey returned, and he escorted Tyler and Kelsey back to the dance floor, with numerous stops to visit guests along the way. When they returned, Kelsey was amused to see a line up of fabulous heels against the base of the stage, and foldable navy ballet flats, the kind that women take when they travel, on many of her guests' feet. Jeffrey had thought of everything.

The DJ was playing slower songs, and Kelsey's ears perked up as she heard the first notes of her favorite Hydronic song, *Chelsea,* start. Suddenly though, the music stopped. Then Kelsey heard someone speak. She looked at the stage and covered her mouth with her hand in shock.

"The boys and I heard that someone very special was getting married here in Port Townsend tonight," said the lead singer of Hydronic, walking out onto the stage, accompanied by his bandmates. "So we thought we'd drop by."

Kelsey looked at Tyler in delight.

"Kelsey Anne, this song is for you," the lead singer continued. The song *Chelsea* began again, and Kelsey swayed in Tyler's arms, but as the band got to the chorus, instead of singing the usual lyrics, they sang,

"Kelsey, Kelsey, Kelsey, you've won my heart."

Kelsey looked at Tyler again, this time in disbelief.

"Kelsey, Kelsey, Kelsey, make my dreams come true," Tyler sang along with the band, and he kissed her hair.

After a fabulous set, Hydronic left the stage and took pictures with Kelsey, Tyler and with their other fans, including Zach. Afterwards, Zach took Kelsey for a quick spin on the dance floor, leaving Tyler to talk to Ryan and Jessica, who had been awakened for cake.

"Having a good time?" Zachary asked, as the DJ began again.

"It's awesome," Kelsey said happily. Tyler's surprise had been amazing.

"Good," Zach said. "The two of you deserve it."

"Thanks," Kelsey said. "Do you really think that Tyler wouldn't have asked me out if you hadn't pushed him?" she asked, referencing Tyler's speech.

"Tyler seems to think so," Zach said with a shrug. "My guess is that it would have taken him a couple of extra months." Zach glanced over at Tyler. "He really loves you, you know."

"I know," Kelsey said with a smile.

After a lovely display of fireworks, and as they waited for the cake to be brought in, Kelsey and Tyler said hello to Alexa — Kimmy and Gareth's almost one-year-old baby. She was the spitting image of Kim, and absolutely delightful.

"She's such a sweetheart," Tyler said, as Kelsey played peekaboo with her. "Nothing like her mother," he added.

"That's what I get for saying nice things about you," Kimmy replied. "I should have told the truth."

Tyler laughed. "It says everything about you that you think that you said nice things about me up there," he replied. Kimmy flipped her long black hair unconcernedly.

Jeffrey walked over.

"I think we're ready," he said to them.

"Bye, Alexa," Kelsey said looking at the baby in Gareth's arms. Alexa gurgled happily.

"When are the two of you coming down to L.A.?" Gareth asked Tyler.

"No idea," Tyler replied. "You'll probably be back sooner, to see the twins."

"I can't wait," Kimmy said happily. "Ryan bear's going to be such a good father."

"We'll see," Tyler replied. He and Kelsey said their goodbyes, and they followed Jeffrey to the wedding cake, which was on the opposite side of the tables, away from the stage.

Kelsey's eyes widened as they got closer. While the dance party had been going on, the wedding crew had clearly been busy setting up more surprises on this side of the venue. Two dozen food trucks were lined up, their serving windows shut, their servers outside. Kelsey guessed that they were waiting until she and Tyler had cut the wedding cake before they opened for business.

Kelsey and Tyler were led to a large table — which featured not only the stunning wedding cake, covered in delicate sugar decorations and with a navy enameled metal K and T cake topper — but also another cake, of a type that Kelsey had only seen in Ballard before — the Norwegian cake that Margaret had promised the couple. It was decorated with both American and Norwegian mini-flags, and looked quite festive.

The master of ceremonies announced the cutting of the cake, and Kelsey was surprised how many of their guests came over to watch. Tyler picked up a silver knife, Kelsey put her hand on top of his, and they cut the cake together.

Kelsey laughed as the two of them attempted to put the chocolate cake neatly on a plate, but they managed. Tyler fed Kelsey the first bite with his fingers, ignoring the forks which lay on the table. She ate it, and reciprocated by offering Tyler a bite of his own. As he did so, he licked a bit of the caramel frosting off her finger and smiled wickedly. Kelsey felt herself blush.

Tyler stepped over to the Norwegian cake, and with Margaret looking on happily, Tyler removed the topmost ring, broke it in half, and offered a bite to Kelsey. She ate it, and wasn't surprised at how delicious it was. She took a piece of the cake from Tyler and offered it to him. He took a bite and the crowd applauded. Tyler took Kelsey's hand, they stepped away from the cake table, and an assistant stepped forward, to finish cutting the cake. As she did so, servers passed out pre-cut servings of the three wedding cakes she and Tyler had selected.

"Thank you for the cake, Margaret," Tyler said to her.

"Yes, thank you," Kelsey agreed.

"Did you like it?" Margaret asked Kelsey.

"It was delicious," Kelsey said, "and so pretty."

"Kelsey wants one for her birthday," Tyler commented. "It's next month."

"Tyler!" Kelsey scolded him. But she had to admit, she sort of did.

"I'm sure I can arrange that," Margaret said happily.

Once the cake was cut, the shutters opened on the food trucks. As some of their older guests said goodbye, Kelsey was able to glance at some of the offerings. There was an traditional ice cream truck, with all of the old-school favorites. On the other hand, there was a food truck offering molecular gastronomy desserts, one of which featured smoke rising from what Kelsey thought was a broken glass sphere, until a guest reached down and tasted a piece of the shards.

"Blown sugar," Tyler mused. He was watching too.

As guests walked by, Kelsey saw cake in jars, popsicles, and giant cookies in their hands. There was a food truck featuring Southeast Asian desserts, and there was a large enough line that extra servers had been dispatched to help. Lisa Olsen was standing by a truck with a giant stick of blue cotton candy, which she was offering to Bill Simon. He shook his head, and Lisa laughed as she ate a piece.

"Kelsey, I'm heading back to the boat," Grandma Rose said, as she walked up to the couple with her assistant. Just as Jeffrey had been assigned to keep track of the wedding couple, Grandma Rose as well as Kelsey's parents, Lisa and Chris had all been given assistants of their own. Kelsey imagined that it was a busy night for them also, since they would have had lists of people to greet, much like Kelsey and Tyler had.

"I'm so glad you were here," Kelsey said.

"Thank you for wearing my dress," Grandma said, holding Kelsey's hands and looking at it. In some ways, it was the most stunning of the three dresses Kelsey had worn tonight. The lace had been removed from Grandma's dress and fashioned into a modern halter top, which was backless and a little daring. Kelsey loved it, and Jeffrey had promised her that he would have it shortened just a tiny bit, so she could wear it again.

"Thank you for giving it to me. It was very special," Kelsey said.

Grandma smiled at her and hugged Tyler.

"Now I have a grandson," Grandma Rose said to him.

"You do," Tyler beamed.

"Your other grandmother is something else. I see where your mother gets her feistiness."

Tyler laughed. "Lisa is nothing compared to my grandmother," he commented.

"I can see that," Grandma agreed. "OK, let me head on."

"Get a good night's sleep," Kelsey said.

Grandma looked at her curiously. "I'm going to the after-party on the cruise ship. I'm heading back early so I can change."

"Oh," Kelsey said. Tyler gave her a grin. "Well, have fun."

"I will, darling. I hope that I see you before Thanksgiving."

"We'll try," Kelsey said, giving her grandmother a final hug. "Have a good night."

"You too," Grandma said as she and her assistant strolled away.

Tyler put his arm around Kelsey's waist. "We should go home too," he said.

Kelsey looked at him curiously.

"I have an after-party planned for us too," he said.

And Kelsey blushed again.

Finally it was time for Kelsey to throw the bouquet. Morgan stood close by with her sisters. Kelsey planned to aim in their direction, but she was a little concerned because Morgan had threatened to let the flowers fall if they were heading her way. Morgan swore that Anna would risk life and limb to catch them, though. Jade took time off from her guarding duties and joined the unmarried women. It gave Tyler a chance to talk to Conor, who Kelsey had barely seen during the event.

Kelsey giggled, turned her back to the large group of women, and threw the rose bouquet as hard as she could behind her. She heard shouts and a scramble, and she turned to see who had caught it. It was her former Darrow classmate, Jen.

Kelsey took a photograph with Jen. Kelsey knew there was a sad irony to Jen catching the bouquet. She had recently broken up with her long-time fiance, having grown tired of waiting for him to finally commit to a wedding date.

"This is a sign that my luck is about to change," Jen said positively as they took the picture.

"Exactly," Kelsey said.

After the bouquet toss, Tyler and Kelsey paused to say goodbye to their parents.

"Nothing better happen to my daughter," Dan North said, a little menacingly, to Tyler. Tyler glanced at Conor, who grinned.

"I can't protect you from angry in-laws," Conor said.

"I'll be fine," Kelsey said, giving her father a hug.

"You'd better be," he replied, glaring at Tyler.

"Have a good honeymoon," Lisa Olsen said, giving Tyler a kiss on the cheek. "I'll see you a week from Monday."

"OK," Tyler said, giving his mother a hug.

"All the best to you, Kelsey," Chris said to her.

"Thanks, Chris," Kelsey replied.

"Maybe I'll see the two of you in New York soon?" he asked, directing the question to Tyler.

"We'll see," Tyler replied, noncommittally. Kelsey made a mental note to convince Tyler to return to New York sometime over the next year. She really wanted Chris and Tyler to get back to a good place.

"Congratulations, Kelsey," Lisa said to her, and Lisa gave her a gentle hug.

"Thank you," Kelsey said in surprise.

A few moments later, Tyler joined Kelsey in a bright red vintage Karmann Ghia convertible, which had been decorated with a large 'Just Married' sign and lots of white streamers. A large crowd of onlookers stood by, holding sparklers. A cheer went up as Tyler started the engine and drove off, and Kelsey waved at the crowd.

"Free," Tyler said, shifting gears.

"It was fun," Kelsey said to him, her blonde hair whipping in the evening wind.

"I can think of things that are much more fun," Tyler replied. Kelsey bit her lip and felt herself blush.

Tyler pulled the sports car up to a curb a few minutes later, and turned off the engine. He took off his seat belt, and looked at Kelsey, who beamed back at him. It had been an incredible day, and as Tyler kissed her, Kelsey knew that she could look forward to a passionate night. However, her reaction to the thought wasn't quite what she expected.

For months she had imagined what it would be like to be Tyler's wife. To be with him every day. And every night. To share the secrets that they hadn't yet shared. But as Kelsey kissed Tyler back, and her held her hands in the darkened car, her anxiety rose.

Kelsey loved Tyler, and she knew that he loved her. She wanted the intimacy that married people shared, and a part of her was surprised that she had managed to wait for so long for him. As a graduate with a Biology degree, Kelsey knew that sex was normal, natural, and necessary — not only for reproduction, but also for emotional bonding.

Yet Kelsey was nervous, and she wasn't quite sure why.

Tyler broke away from her, and looked into her eyes with his own. His eyes sparkled in the moonlight.

"Should we go inside?" he asked her. Kelsey nodded at him. Tyler smiled at her and kissed her once again. He opened his car door and stepped out into the street, closing the door behind himself. Kelsey removed her seat belt, but waited in her seat. She knew that Tyler would want to help the once-again heel-clad Kelsey out of the car. She had changed shoes right before throwing the bouquet.

Tyler opened Kelsey's door, and extended his hand down to her. She took it and allowed Tyler to help her stand. He surveyed her for a moment, then closed her car door. Then Kelsey took his arm, and Tyler led her up the path to the former Seaforth house.

Kelsey looked at it in the dark. It was a beautiful Victorian home, built on not one, but two large lots. And now it was hers. Her eyes took in the beautiful manicured lawn, the large covered porch, and the elegant rosebushes that lined the house.

"Will this be OK for the night?" Tyler asked Kelsey.

"It's perfect," Kelsey said, nuzzling him. Despite her anxious feelings about the evening's agenda, Kelsey felt nothing but love for Tyler.

Her new husband.

At the foot of the stairs, Tyler turned to Kelsey, and without warning scooped her up into his arms. Kelsey threw her arms around his neck in surprise.

"What are you doing?" she asked, as Tyler carried her up the stairs.

"Carrying you over the threshold," Tyler replied. He stepped onto the porch, and nudged the front door with his foot. It swung open, and Tyler carried Kelsey inside.

He kissed her, and set her down carefully. Kelsey gave him a gentle hug, and he hugged back. They clung to each other in the softly lit foyer of the house, and they gave each other kisses.

"Welcome home," Tyler said to Kelsey.

"Home is where you are," Kelsey replied, cuddling against him. Tyler sighed happily. He led her over to the living room, and they sat on the sofa together. Kelsey leaned against him peacefully, and Tyler put his arm around her shoulder.

Kelsey looked up at Tyler. "Did you have fun?" she asked.

"What do you think?" Tyler replied.

"We're married," she said, nuzzling against him again.

"That we are, Princess," Tyler replied, kissing her hair. "So today was a good day."

"Just good?" Kelsey teased.

"The best of my life," Tyler corrected.

"Mine too," Kelsey said, kissing him. The couple sat together in silence for a moment, then Tyler shifted, and reached down to Kelsey's feet. He slipped the straps off of her ankles, and the shoes fell to the living room carpet.

"Thank you," Kelsey said. She wiggled her polished toes, and pulled her legs up under herself. Tyler took her back into his arms and kissed her hair.

Kelsey reached out, and took Tyler's left hand into her own. She smiled at the gold band encircling his ring finger, and placed her own ring finger next to his.

"A matched set," Kelsey said happily. Tyler kissed her again. They sat together on the sofa, Tyler holding Kelsey, and Kelsey delighting in his love. She glanced up at him, and he looked back at her with a happy smile on his face.

"What?" Kelsey asked. But of course she knew why he was happy.

"I just can't believe I'm married to you," Tyler admitted.

"You'll believe it in a few days, when you're tired of me," Kelsey teased.

"I will never be tired of you," Tyler said happily. Kelsey reached up and stroked his face. "But I am getting tired. Do you want to go upstairs?" he asked.

Kelsey froze. She did and she didn't.

This must have been what Jess felt like, she thought, but the knowledge didn't make her feel better.

Kelsey sighed to herself, and stood up with determination.

"Let's go," she said.

Kelsey and Tyler held hands as they walked up the staircase. White rose petals caressed the soles of Kelsey's bare feet as she stepped on them. Someone had created a trail from the front door to the master bedroom, Kelsey realized as they walked into the room.

"Have you been in the house before?" Kelsey asked.

"No," Tyler replied. "Have you?"

"No. I didn't know the Seaforth family," Kelsey replied. She looked around the enormous bedroom and bit her lip as she looked at the king size bed. Tyler released her hand, and sat on the edge of the bed. He loosened his tie and looked up at her. Kelsey felt her heart pound. She spotted her bag sitting on the dresser and she walked over to it. Kelsey rummaged around the bag, looking for the lingerie pouch holding her trousseau. Suddenly, she felt Tyler's hands around her waist. He kissed her neck, and she felt the gentle rise and fall of his chest on her back.

"I love you so much," he whispered. Kelsey closed her eyes.

"Me, too," she said softly. Tyler held her for another moment, then he released her, and Kelsey resumed looking for the small pouch. She found it, and pulled it out with her manicured hands. Without looking at Tyler, she headed for the en-suite bathroom.

"Wait," Tyler said. Kelsey paused, bare feet on the soft carpet. She felt Tyler's hand at the base of her neck. "May I?" he asked.

"Yes," Kelsey replied breathlessly. Then without another word, Tyler unbuttoned the neck of Kelsey's dress. His hands gently caressed her back.

"Thank you," Kelsey said abruptly, and she hurried to the bathroom.

She tried to calm her breathing as she leaned against the closed door. The painted wood felt cool against her warm back. Kelsey stood for a moment, and tried to pinpoint the cause of her her anxiety, but after a moment, she realized that it was simply that she was about to do something that she had never done before.

Something meaningful, with the love of her life.

Kelsey cursed her nerves, reached behind her back, and unzipped her dress at the waist. She took it off, and lay the dress onto the spacious counter. Kelsey looked at her made-up face in the mirror. Tania's handiwork had remained flawless. Kelsey pondered herself for a moment, then she picked up a washcloth.

It took a while for Kelsey to muster the courage to leave the bathroom once she was dressed, but finally she decided that she could no longer keep her husband waiting. She nervously put her hand on the doorknob and walked back into the bedroom. While Kelsey had been in the bathroom, Tyler had shed his own clothes, which sat in a heap on one of the chairs. He sat once again on the edge of the bed, wearing nothing but a pair of black boxer briefs. He smiled at Kelsey.

"You look beautiful," he said, and despite her fears, Kelsey smiled. Tyler rose to meet her. As he stood before her, Kelsey fumbled with the silk belt tied at her waist, and after what felt like a long time, she untied it. The belt released, and Kelsey's cream-colored satin robe fell open.

Tyler slid a finger down a tendril of her long blonde hair, as Kelsey removed the robe from her shoulders. Tyler leaned down and kissed her right shoulder. Kelsey closed her eyes. Bliss mixed with nerves and she took a deep breath as Tyler placed his arms around her waist and pulled her towards himself. He covered her with kisses, as Kelsey's heart began to pound again. The silk robe slid to the floor.

Tyler looked into Kelsey's eyes, kissed her neck, then he reached his hand to the silk ribbon on her shoulder.

"I finally get to see you in a teddy," Tyler commented. Kelsey nodded without speaking. Tyler slipped a finger through the bow of the ribbon, and tugged at it. The bow undid itself, and Kelsey's shoulder was completely bare. Tyler repeated the gesture on the other side, and the top of the silk teddy slid to the top of Kelsey's chest. Kelsey felt herself beginning to blush.

Tyler surveyed Kelsey with his smoldering brown eyes. He placed his hands on the silk fabric around her waist, and with a swift movement, tugged it down. The satin teddy fell to the floor and puddled around Kelsey's ankles.

Kelsey knew her face was bright red as she stood naked before Tyler, but he had taken her hands into his own, and was surveying the parts of Kelsey that had been a mystery to him until now. He looked up at her face, and Kelsey watched as his face changed from pleased to questioning. Kelsey turned away, shyly. Tyler looked puzzled for a moment, then he pulled her hand up to his lips and kissed it.

"Thank you for waiting for me," he said softly. Kelsey continued to look away, but nodded. "Come," Tyler said, pulling her gently to the large bed.

Kelsey felt like her heart was going to explode, as she sat on the bed, then lay down. Then her eyes widened in surprise, as Tyler pulled a soft sheet over her naked body. He lay next to her and propped himself on a pillow. He smiled down at her.

"We can wait," he said simply. He ran his finger through her hair again. "We have a lifetime together."

Kelsey looked into his gentle brown eyes. There was no disappointment there, nothing but love. She considered his words.

"No," Kelsey said firmly. "I'll be just as nervous tomorrow."

"Are you sure?" Tyler asked.

"Positive," Kelsey replied.

Tyler looked at her thoughtfully. "Tell you what," Tyler said. "Let's see what you like. If you don't like something, or you want to stop, you say the word, and we'll stop."

"OK," Kelsey replied. She took a breath. She had been more anxious than she realized. Kelsey had no idea why. She was with Tyler, he was her husband, and she was safe and loved.

"Promise you'll be honest with me," Tyler said. "We're doing this together."

Kelsey smiled through her nerves, which were lessening.

"I promise," she replied. Tyler surveyed her for another moment, then he kissed her on the lips.

"OK," he said. He slipped his arm around Kelsey's bare shoulders, and for a moment, Kelsey thought he was going to change his mind and suggest that they go to sleep, but instead he nuzzled against her, and kissed her neck. Kelsey closed her eyes and relaxed with his touch.

Tyler gently slid the sheet off Kelsey's shoulders. The fabric rested on the base of her collarbone, and she breathed deeply. Kelsey felt her anxiety shifting to a different feeling.

Excitement.

She shivered with the soft touch of his lips against her skin, as Tyler leaned into her as he reached across her body and caressed her bare arm with his hand. Kelsey smiled, as he kissed her again and again.

After a while, Tyler paused. He looked at her, and Kelsey kissed him on the lips. Tyler looked at her, a bit mischievously, then he slid the sheet to her hips. And Kelsey took another deep breath.

Tyler caressed Kelsey with his hands, kissed her with his lips, tasted her with his mouth. Kelsey reached out and stroked his face at moments, and Tyler returned to her lips for kisses. But it was clear to Kelsey that tonight Tyler's goal was to learn how to pleasure his new wife, and always, Tyler was a very focused scholar.

Kelsey felt herself go from warm, to hot, to boiling in a moment. The sheet had been tossed aside.

"Tyler," Kelsey breathed.

"Yes," Tyler said unconcernedly, kissing her upper thigh.

"Tyler," Kelsey said more urgently. In the moment, she had lost her ability to put words together. She supposed Tyler would figure out what she meant. She looked at him as her bare chest rose and fell. Tyler's brown eyes shone, and he smiled at his bride.

In a flash, Tyler removed his lone piece of clothing. Kelsey reached up to him, and pulled Tyler towards herself.

And for the first time, they were one.

Kelsey turned sleepily as sunbeams shone into the bedroom. For a fleeting second, Kelsey wondered why Tyler's arms were around her, then she smiled and cuddled against his warm body.

"Good morning, beautiful," Tyler said, kissing her.

"Good morning," Kelsey replied joyfully.

"How is my bride this morning?"

"Happy."

"That's what I want to hear," Tyler said, tightening his grasp around her body. He nuzzled her hair, which was splayed over the soft pillow.

"And how is my groom?"

"I have no words," Tyler said. Kelsey giggled and stroked his cheek with her hand. Tyler looked at her with his sparkling brown eyes. As always, Tyler looked delicious when he first woke up.

"Should we get up?" Kelsey asked him.

"I never want to leave this bed," Tyler replied.

Kelsey giggled again. "We have to sometime," she said.

"No we don't," Tyler said, pulling her towards him and kissing her.

Kelsey took a deep breath.

"I suppose we don't," she conceded, as she kissed Tyler back.

Two hours later, Kelsey woke up again. Tyler was fast asleep. Kelsey gently moved Tyler's arms from around her body, but her movement woke him, and he opened his eyes.

"Sorry," Kelsey said, kissing him on the lips.

Tyler kissed her back, then yawned. "It's fine," he said. "Athena, what time is it?"

"The time is 11:23 a.m.," said a computerized voice in the room.

Kelsey was startled for a moment, then she realized that of course Tyler's home would have every bit of technology that Tactec produced. Tyler smiled at Kelsey.

"Are you hungry?" she asked him.

"Hungry for you," Tyler replied. Kelsey blushed and Tyler kissed her on the nose. "Perhaps you need a bit of food, though," he conceded. "We have gotten quite a bit of exercise."

Kelsey blushed a bit deeper. Tyler laughed and gave her a hug. Kelsey leaned on him peacefully, blissfully. Breakfast could wait.

"I don't think we can call this breakfast any more," Tyler said, sitting across from Kelsey at the kitchen table a while later.

"Probably not," Kelsey agreed. She picked up a warm scone and broke it in half. The satin sleeve of her robe slid down her arm. Kelsey looked at the scone curiously after she tasted it.

"Ben made these?" she asked.

Tyler winked at her. "I got him a catering job," he commented. "Everyone on the cruise ship had them for breakfast this morning."

"That was nice of you." Kelsey said, taking another bite of scone.

Tyler shook his head. "Nice? I think profitable is the correct word," he replied. Kelsey giggled. Of course, Tyler was still part owner of Ben's cafe.

"Did you at least give Jeffrey a discount?" Kelsey asked.

"Of course not. I told Ben to hike up the price," Tyler replied.

"You're quite the businessman," Kelsey said.

"Thank you," Tyler said, biting into his own scone.

"So what else are we doing today?" Kelsey asked, eating a chocolate chip.

Tyler smiled seductively.

"'Else' was the important word," Kelsey replied.

Tyler glanced around the room.

"We can take a tour of your new estate," he commented.

"It's really big," Kelsey said.

Tyler nodded. "Lisa did a good job picking it out," he said.

Kelsey looked at Tyler curiously. "Lisa? You didn't help?"

Tyler shook his head. "I didn't know about it until last week," he replied.

"So where are we going to honeymoon?" Kelsey asked.

"You'll see. We still have three nights until you have to go back to work."

Kelsey smiled. Tyler obviously had a surprise planned.

"When do we leave?"

Tyler thought for a moment.

"Tomorrow morning," he said. "If that's OK with my bride?"

"Maybe," Kelsey said. "I might want to sleep late," she added seductively.

"Anything for my princess," Tyler replied huskily. He reached out, pulled her hand to his lips, and kissed Kelsey's fingertips.

Kelsey looked into Tyler's eyes, and felt herself fall under his spell once again.

"Anything?" she asked breathlessly.

"Anything at all," Tyler replied, kissing her palm. Kelsey glanced at him, and pulled her hand away from him.

"Am I making you uncomfortable, Mrs. Olsen?" Tyler teased. Kelsey pulled her eyes up to meet his. She nodded without taking her eyes off him.

Tyler stood up from his chair and walked over to her. Tyler knelt next to her, put his hand behind her head, and kissed her hard. Kelsey looped her arms around his neck, Tyler lifted her out of the chair, and as he carried her out of the room, Kelsey sighed happily.

"Athena, what time is it?" Kelsey called out.

"The time is 4:57 p.m."

Kelsey turned toward Tyler, who was lying in bed next to her. He smiled at her.

"Here we are again," Kelsey commented. Tyler laughed delightedly and kissed her.

"Is that a problem?" Tyler asked.

"It wouldn't be, but now I'm starving. For food," Kelsey quickly added.

"I don't think you finished your scone," Tyler commented.

"Yeah, I'm pretty sure I didn't," Kelsey replied, sitting up in bed.

"We could try to eat breakfast again," Tyler said.

"At 4:57 p.m.," Kelsey said.

"Breakfast is served all day," Tyler teased.

Kelsey giggled and fell back onto Tyler. "This is crazy," she commented.

"What's crazy?" Tyler asked.

"How much I love you," Kelsey replied.

Tyler wrapped his arms around Kelsey and nuzzled her ear.

"OK, we're getting up."

"OK," Tyler said.

Kelsey pushed Tyler away. "I mean out of bed," she said, sitting upright again.

"I knew that," Tyler said.

"I thought I needed to make myself clear after the past eighteen hours," Kelsey replied. She reached down next to the bed, and picked up her silk robe. She put it on as she sat on the bed. She glanced at Tyler.

"Come on, let's go," Kelsey said.

"Actually, I thought I'd stay here. Save us a few minutes the next time you decide to drag me to bed," Tyler replied.

"'Drag you to bed?'" Kelsey repeated.

Tyler smiled, crossed his arms behind his head and leaned back on his pillow.

Kelsey surveyed him for a moment.

"Fine, you're right. You're irresistible," she conceded. "But get up anyway. We're going to try to eat breakfast again."

"If you say so, Mrs. Olsen," Tyler said, sitting up. Tyler ran his hand through his chestnut-brown hair, and Kelsey pulled her eyes away from him. She bit her lip and stood up quickly. She was starving, but Tyler was completely tempting.

Kelsey waited as Tyler pulled on pajama pants, then she took his hand as they walked out of bedroom and back down the stairs. They stopped in the downstairs bathroom to wash their hands, then headed back to the kitchen. Their half-eaten scones sat on the kitchen table. Kelsey walked over and picked hers up. She took a bite.

"Do you want something else?" Tyler asked, picking up his own.

"After I finish this, I do," Kelsey said. She sat back down in her chair and crossed her legs. Tyler stood next to her, watching her.

"What?" Kelsey asked, licking chocolate off her finger.

Tyler bit his lip and turned away.

Kelsey was puzzled for a moment, then she smiled.

"Tempted, Mr. Olsen?" she asked.

"Quiet. That is, if you want to eat," Tyler replied. Kelsey giggled and broke off another piece of scone. Tyler walked to the refrigerator and leaned against the counter.

"I seem to have an audience," Kelsey commented, popping the piece of scone into her mouth.

"I like watching you eat," Tyler replied. "It's very sexy."

"Is it?" Kelsey asked, tossing her hair back.

Tyler grinned at her. "Keep tempting fate, Mrs. Olsen. The bedroom's just steps away."

"Are you going to seduce me again?" Kelsey asked.

"Just say the word," Tyler replied.

Kelsey smiled and turned back to her scone.

"It will have to wait. I'm starving. What else is there?" Kelsey asked.

Tyler opened the fridge. "Pesto lasagna, mushroom risotto, and tortellini," Tyler replied.

"Margaret?" Kelsey asked.

"Ryan," Tyler said, closing the fridge.

"Really?" Kelsey said. "That was nice."

"He's freezing meals for when Jess has the babies," Tyler said. "Which one do you want?"

"Tortellini," Kelsey said.

"How hungry are you?" Tyler asked.

"Super hungry," Kelsey said.

"I'll microwave it then," Tyler said, re-opening the fridge and pulling out two containers.

"Thanks," Kelsey said, finishing the scone. She took a sip of the water that was sitting on the table.

Tyler placed a container in the microwave, pressed the button, then joined Kelsey at the table.

"Think you can keep your hands off me long enough to eat?" Kelsey asked.

"I think I should be asking you that," Tyler retorted.

"You probably should," Kelsey conceded. She stretched out her leg and rubbed it against Tyler's.

"There you go again," Tyler said with a grin.

Kelsey shrugged. "My hands aren't on you," she said. "Yet," she added.

Tyler's grin grew wider. "I'm starting to understand why you wouldn't sleep with me in law school," he said.

"Why?" Kelsey asked curiously.

"We wouldn't have graduated," Tyler replied. "We would have always been in bed."

Kelsey winked at him. "See? It's good that we waited."

Tyler reached down, and rubbed Kelsey's ankle with his hand. The microwave beeped.

"Your food's ready," Tyler said.

"And?" Kelsey said.

"I thought you were hungry," Tyler commented.

Kelsey moved her leg away from Tyler's. "I am." she said.

Tyler stood and walked over to the microwave. He opened it, stirred the contents of the container, and closed the microwave again. He pressed the button, and set the spoon he had used on a plate.

"I think I'll stay over here," Tyler said.

"That's probably best," Kelsey admitted.

After they finished breakfast at 5:30 p.m., Kelsey and Tyler walked hand in hand back up to the bedroom. They had decided to go outside, to the beautiful backyard, and enjoy the summer sun for a while.

Kelsey walked over to her open travel bag. As she rummaged around it looking for her new bikini, she moved several pieces of lingerie around. Lingerie was very new to her, as she had never really given her undergarments any attention. Kelsey had been surprised that she liked wearing the lacy, silky pieces. And Tyler seemed to like them too.

Kelsey finally found the white bikini, and pulled the top and bottom out of her bag. She replaced the lingerie pieces that she had displaced. She would need them later.

Kelsey turned around, her bikini in her hand. She read the look in Tyler's eyes.

"I think I'll change in the bathroom." Kelsey said.

"We're married," Tyler pouted.

Kelsey giggled. She walked over and gave him a kiss.

"See you in a minute," she replied, walking into the bathroom and closing the door.

Kelsey took a quick shower, then put on her bikini. She fluffed her hair as she looked at herself in the mirror. As she did so, she pondered whether she looked different as a married woman, no longer an innocent girl. Kelsey supposed not. She had never thought of herself as particularly innocent. She took one more look in the mirror, and stepped back out into the bedroom.

Tyler was lying on the bed, looking at his phone. He was wearing a pair of navy-blue swim trunks. He glanced up as Kelsey walked back into the room.

"Is that new?" he asked. Kelsey nodded. She was wearing a white crocheted string bikini, which she had purchased online. When she had tried it on at home, she realized that it left little to the imagination, which made it perfect for lying in the backyard, and inappropriate for virtually everywhere else.

"Did you buy it for me?" Tyler asked.

"I bought it because I needed a bikini," Kelsey countered.

"I see," Tyler said thoughtfully.

Kelsey watched in amusement as Tyler's eyes scanned her. "I thought we were going outside," she said.

"What? Right, I guess we were," Tyler said, standing.

"Are you OK?" Kelsey asked.

"You distracted me," Tyler replied.

"Me or the bikini?" Kelsey asked.

"What bikini?" Tyler asked. Kelsey gave him a smile. Tyler put his arm around Kelsey's bare waist and gave her a kiss.

Kelsey took his hand, and led him downstairs. They walked to the back door of the house and stepped out onto the back porch.

"This is really beautiful," Kelsey said, as they stood hand in hand, overlooking the backyard. The backyard was sectioned into three different areas. One was a large flower garden, which could be seen from the street. The second part was a tiny cottage, which had a cozy seating area outside, and the third area was designed for entertaining, with lounge chairs and an outdoor kitchen with barbecue.

"I wonder what's in the cottage?" Tyler asked.

Kelsey glanced at him.

"I haven't planned a surprise, Princess. I was just wondering," Tyler clarified.

"Let's go look there first," Kelsey said. "Do you think we need shoes?" she asked. Both of them were barefoot.

"I'll get some," Tyler said. He kissed her hand and walked back into the house. Kelsey surveyed the yard as the warm summer breeze wafted over her.

"Wow," Kelsey said. She turned back to the house and looked up at it. Tyler came back out, holding two pairs of flip-flops. He handed the pair of white sparkly ones to Kelsey. They said 'Bride' on the sole. Kelsey looked at Tyler curiously.

"Where did you get these?" she asked.

Tyler grinned mischievously. "You'll need them for the second half of our honeymoon," he said mysteriously.

"Fine," Kelsey said, putting the flip-flops on. Tyler put his on, and they walked down the stairs of the porch and over to the cottage.

A key on a navy ribbon was in the lock of the large French doors. Kelsey turned it and opened the door. She gasped in delight.

"It's so cute!" she said excitedly, turning to Tyler.

"Nice," Tyler agreed. Kelsey turned back to the cottage. Inside was a warmly-decorated space, also perfect for entertaining. A game table was surrounded by chairs, a bookcase had stacks of games and outdoor play equipment, and a projector hung from the ceiling, ready for movie night.

A bar at the other end of the cottage sported a popcorn maker, as well as a mini-soft ice cream dispenser. The decor was modern, and held several personal touches including strings of the customized Christmas tree ornaments that Tyler had given her over the years, along with a Darrow Law banner.

Kelsey hugged Tyler, teary-eyed.

"Thank you," she said.

"We'll have to thank Jeffrey," Tyler commented. "This has his fingerprints all over it."

Kelsey looked at the miniature "Chelsea" sign that was on the wall closest to her.

"How did he have time to arrange this?" Kelsey asked.

"No idea," Tyler replied.

"I could stay here all day," Kelsey said, looking around. Suddenly, something shiny outside the window caught her eye.

"What's that?" Kelsey asked, pulling Tyler's hand and heading back outside.

An Airstream trailer sat in the driveway next to the house.

"I guess they decided not to take it to Medina," Tyler said of the trailer that he and his groomsmen had got dressed in.

"I guess not," Kelsey said. "Come on. Let's sit in the sun."

She turned back to the cottage, took another long look around, and locked it with the key. She gave the key to Tyler.

"I don't have anywhere to put this," she said.

"I can see that," Tyler replied, taking the key from her. He leaned down and kissed her neck. Kelsey felt a spark run through her body. She was feeling hot, and Kelsey knew it had nothing to do with the summer sun.

They walked over to the outdoor seating area. Tyler tossed the key on a side table, and Kelsey lay out on one of the chaise lounges. She smiled blissfully. She heard the sound of a piece of furniture being moved, and glanced at Tyler. The other chaise nudged hers, and Tyler lay on it.

"That's better," he said, glancing at her. "I'll have to tell Jeffrey we want a double one. I'm surprised he didn't think of it."

Kelsey gave Tyler a look.

"Double chaises are like a bed. I bet he thought it wasn't a good idea," she commented.

Tyler smiled at her. "It's a great idea." He leaned over, wrapped his arm around her waist, and kissed her.

"Tyler, we're outside," Kelsey warned.

"I don't see anyone," Tyler replied. "And there's a fence."

"Stay on your side," Kelsey said.

Tyler leaned a bit closer to Kelsey — then, without warning, he pulled her on top of himself.

"Tyler!" Kelsey protested. But she didn't move.

"You said to stay on my side," Tyler replied, kissing her. His sexy eyes looked into hers. "This is a good spot for you."

"I bet you think so," Kelsey commented. She ran her hands down his muscular arms.

"I bet you do too," Tyler said seductively.

Kelsey's breathing was getting faster. "We've only been outside for five minutes," she said.

"Outside will be here later," Tyler replied, pulling her tightly and kissing her. Kelsey closed her eyes, as Tyler stroked her bare back.

"I thought we were coming out to be in the sun," Kelsey said weakly. Tyler had tugged on the tie of her string bikini bottom and loosened one side. He ran his hand down her thigh.

"Haven't you had enough time outside?" Tyler asked huskily. "I think it's time to go back in." He leaned next to her ear. "Learn a few more things about each other," he whispered.

Kelsey's chest rose and fell, in sync with Tyler's. She opened her eyes and looked at him.

"You win," she said.

"I know," Tyler replied with a kiss.

"Athena, I don't want to know what time it is," Kelsey said.

A green light shone briefly in the dark room.

"The time is 9:38 p.m."

"It's a software bug. She doesn't listen to everything you say," Tyler said, stroking Kelsey's hair. She snuggled up against his bare chest.

"Neither do you," Kelsey said.

Tyler laughed. "What have I missed?" Tyler asked.

"The part where I said we should spend the evening outside."

"It seems to me that you weren't listening to yourself either. I didn't exactly drag you inside."

"Details," Kelsey said.

"Don't worry, Princess. You'll have plenty of opportunities to be outside tomorrow," Tyler said, as he held her in his arms.

"You still won't tell me where we're going?"

"No. But if you think about it, you'll already know," Tyler replied.

Kelsey thought for a moment. "Vancouver?" she asked.

"See, you already knew," Tyler replied.

"No," Kelsey pouted. "I'm not going to Vancouver."

"Why?" Tyler asked in surprise.

"I want to stay here with you. Vancouver is almost a four-hour drive away," Kelsey replied. She didn't say what she was thinking, which was that they hadn't managed to be out of the bedroom for more than an hour since they had arrived in the house. There was no way she wanted to spend four hours in a car, sitting next to Tyler, but unable to cuddle with him. She was already dreading going back to work.

"We won't drive there," Tyler said, stroking her naked back. "It's fine."

"Even if we fly, we have to drive, right?" Kelsey asked.

"You're really impatient," Tyler commented.

"I'm just trying to understand how we're getting there," she said thoughtfully. "If we fly, we have to drive to the airport, fly up to Vancouver, then drive from the airport to the hotel."

"I suppose that's true."

Kelsey knew that there was no bed on Bob's small plane, and Kelsey wasn't sure if Bob still had that plane anyway, now that Morgan was gone.

"That's a lot of time out of bed," Kelsey finally commented.

Tyler burst out laughing.

"I'm only thinking of you," Kelsey added.

"Right," Tyler said as he laughed. After a moment, he gained control of himself and reached for his phone. "Tell you what Princess, let's leave now," he said, typing on his phone in the darkened room.

"Now?" Kelsey said.

"Yes, now. Then you'll see how we're getting there."

Kelsey smiled. She was satisfied. Her impatience was about to be rewarded.

Tyler took a quick shower — which he invited Kelsey to join in — but Kelsey declined, choosing to pack instead. She put away her lingerie, packed her dress, and placed everything into her bag, except the summer dress she would wear to Vancouver, and the flip-flops that Tyler had given her. Kelsey stood in the room, wondering if she had missed anything, as Tyler walked in, wrapped in a towel. He smiled at her wickedly. Kelsey was only wearing her underwear.

"We're leaving," Kelsey said, addressing him.

"Let's hurry," Tyler replied. With a wink, he dropped his towel.

And Kelsey smiled.

"It didn't take long for you to get comfortable with me," Tyler said as they drove down Monroe Street.

Kelsey looked at him curiously, then she understood.

"I suppose it didn't. I've been lusting after you for a long time," Kelsey admitted.

"Have you?"

"Yep," Kelsey said, and she realized that it was completely true. Once the intimacy barrier between them had been broken, so had Kelsey's shyness. As Tyler's wife, she felt as comfortable with him about sex as she was with virtually everything else.

"Good," Tyler said. "Because I've been lusting after you too."

"Actually, I knew that," Kelsey pointed out.

"I knew too. That you lusted after me, I mean."

"You did not," Kelsey said. "I've hidden it well."

"That's what you think," Tyler replied. "I've seen you looking at me. Undressing me with your beautiful eyes."

Kelsey giggled. "I thought I was being coy," she teased.

"You were wrong," Tyler said.

"It doesn't matter. We're married now. You can know the truth," Kelsey said breezily. "Where are we going?" she asked as the waterfront shone in the darkness before them.

"We're here," Tyler replied, pulling the car into a empty space on the street.

A few minutes later, Kelsey smiled with glee as the boat tender sped towards Bob's yacht. Tyler had thought of everything.

"We were going to have a romantic daylight cruise up to Vancouver," Tyler commented once they were on board the yacht. "But since my bride only wants to hop from bed to bed, I'll tell the captain to get going."

"Your bride only wants to hop from bed to bed? I think you mean my groom," Kelsey said.

"Actually, I was giving you credit for the idea. It sounds perfect to me," Tyler said, wrapping his arms around Kelsey.

She giggled. "Me, too. I'll take credit."

"Once we dock, it's a 10-minute ride to our house. Can you keep your hands off me for that long?" Tyler asked.

"Probably not," Kelsey admitted.

"Good," Tyler said. "I don't want you to get bored with me."

"I'm quite sure that's not going to be a problem, Mr. Olsen. You've managed to keep me pretty excited so far," Kelsey replied.

"I could excite you again," Tyler said softly, kissing her collarbone.

"I bet you can," Kelsey said, closing her eyes happily.

Hours later, Kelsey woke up in Tyler's arms. She glanced at him in the moonlight. He was looking at her in the darkness.

"Hi," Kelsey said, smiling at him.

"Hi, beautiful."

"How long have you been looking at me?" she asked.

"No idea," Tyler said, stroking her face with his hand.

"Athena, what time is it?" Kelsey asked.

"There's no Athena on the yacht," Tyler commented.

"Really? Why?" Kelsey said in surprise.

"Bob likes his privacy."

"I see. Do you know what time it is?" Kelsey asked.

"No."

"Can you look at your phone?"

"No. I left it in Port Townsend."

"You did?" Kelsey asked. She was almost never without her phone. "By accident?"

"It's a Tactec company phone. I'm not allowed to take it over the border," Tyler replied.

"Why not?" Kelsey asked, turning slightly to get more comfortable in Tyler's arms.

"Customs and Border Patrol started searching and seizing cell phones and laptops years ago. Tactec employees are not allowed to take any electronics that they use at the workplace across the border."

"You're a U.S. citizen," Kelsey said, confused.

"We have limited rights at the border, Kels."

"I had no idea," Kelsey said. "Couldn't you just refuse to give them your password?"

"Obviously you've never been detained at the border," Tyler replied.

"No, I haven't," Kelsey agreed. She turned, reached over to the nightstand, and picked up her own phone. She blinked at the bright light. "Sorry," she said, replacing the phone.

"What time is it?" Tyler asked.

"Time for you to kiss me," Kelsey replied, getting comfortable in his arms again.

Tyler kissed Kelsey. "So when do I get my thousand kisses?" he asked.

"You aren't going to give up, are you?" Kelsey asked.

"I've been asking for years," Tyler replied.

"OK. Not today. Maybe not this week. But I promise you that I'll give you a thousand kisses."

"Over the next fifty years?"

"No. In one day," Kelsey said.

"Really?" Tyler said.

"Really," Kelsey started doing the math in her head. *One kiss a minute for a full day.* "On a Sunday."

"OK," Tyler said delightedly. He shifted his arm and pulled Kelsey closer. She reached out and took his left hand into her own. Their wedding rings gently clinked together. She snuggled against him in the dark. She loved their new intimacy. Not just the sex, but the closeness. Skin against skin, no awkwardness, no boundaries. It was magical.

"I could give you a thousand kisses," Tyler commented.

"I'm pretty sure you already have," Kelsey said, thinking about the previous night. "But you could do it again."

"Anytime, Princess," Tyler said. He kissed her bare collarbone. "One," he counted.

Kelsey giggled, turned in his arms, and faced him. She stroked his face with her hand. Tyler had shaved when he had taken his shower, so his face was still smooth. She put her leg on top of his. Tyler ran his hand down her thigh.

Kelsey felt her heart beat faster.

"You're irresistible. You know that, right?" she breathed.

"You think?" Tyler asked. He put his hand on the back of her thigh and pulled Kelsey closer. He kissed her neck. Kelsey arched her back and pressed into him. Tyler responded by stroking her back with his hand.

"I know," Kelsey said, kissing him.

"Do you want your thousand kisses now?" Tyler asked huskily.

"I think I'd rather have something else," Kelsey replied with a smile.

"You know," Tyler said thoughtfully as the sun shone into the windows of the yacht, "I'm starting to think that you married me for my body."

Kelsey giggled and bit into a piece of toast. The staff had left breakfast outside their door.

"And how would you feel about that?" she asked.

"Pretty good, actually," Tyler admitted. He reached out and stroked Kelsey's back. She felt his fingers through the silk fabric of her short robe.

"Want a bite?" Kelsey asked, holding out her toast. Tyler lifted himself up and took a small bite of toast. "I'm glad they fed us. I'm starving."

"You haven't been making time to eat," Tyler commented.

"No, food hasn't been a priority this weekend," Kelsey agreed, taking another bite of toast. She stroked Tyler's bare foot with her own. She frowned. "I don't want to go back to work," she said.

"Don't. Tell Simon you quit," Tyler replied.

Kelsey glanced at him. "If you were going to be at home, I'd consider it," she replied.

"Don't tease me. You'd last for maybe for a day or two, then you'd tell me you were going back to work," Tyler said.

"I don't know. You're pretty tempting," Kelsey said. She put the toast down on the plate and leaned back against Tyler.

"Kelsey, if I thought you were going to stay home, I'd tell Lisa to find another CEO," Tyler commented. "Then I could stay in bed with you."

Kelsey was thoughtful. "I'm sorry I'm not like that," she said.

"Don't be. I like how driven you are."

"Do you?"

"I like everything about you."

"You say that now," Kelsey said.

"I say that always."

"We haven't been married for even 48 hours," Kelsey pointed out.

"I'm confident," Tyler replied.

"Interesting," Kelsey said. She sat back up and took a piece of bacon off the plate. "How much longer to Vancouver?"

"Ready to switch beds?" Tyler asked.

"I don't know. This one's pretty comfortable," Kelsey said. She crossed her legs and took a bite of bacon. "Where are we staying in Vancouver?"

"It's a surprise."

"Another one?"

"You love my surprises," Tyler said.

"I guess," Kelsey said doubtfully. "You said I would need my flip-flops, so I'm guessing it's near the beach." Kelsey glanced at Tyler, who looked back at her innocently.

"Fine," Kelsey said, eating the bacon again.

"You're really impatient," Tyler said.

"I thought you loved everything about me," Kelsey replied.

"I didn't say I didn't like it. I just said it was true," Tyler said.

"I see," Kelsey replied. She finished the bacon, and wiped her hands on a white napkin. She licked her lips and caught Tyler looking at her. He had a sexy grin on his face.

"Mr. Olsen?" Kelsey said sweetly. "Did you have something to share?"

"I have many things to share, Mrs. Olsen," Tyler replied. Kelsey blushed, but gave him a smile.

"It was nice having you back on board, Mrs. Olsen," the captain of the yacht said to Kelsey as her bags and Tyler's were loaded into a waiting town car. Once again in Canada, they were berthed in a marina that could hold Bob's enormous yacht.

"I had a wonderful time," Kelsey said. "Thank you."

Tyler shook the captain's hand, and Tyler and Kelsey walked off the yacht, holding hands. Their chauffeur held the door open for Kelsey, and she got in, with Tyler following. Tyler closed the door and looked at her.

"I'm setting a timer for ten minutes," she said.

Tyler gave her a puzzled look.

"That's how long you said it would take to drive to our hotel," Kelsey reminded him.

Tyler grinned. "Do you have plans for me, Mrs. Olsen?"

"I always have plans for you, Mr. Olsen," Kelsey replied.

Tyler grinned wider.

"Put on your seat belt," Kelsey said, as she put on her own.

Tyler did. "Yes, ma'am," he teased.

Kelsey glanced at him. "You knew I was bossy," she commented.

"True," Tyler said, as the car pulled away. Kelsey glanced out the window, at the sparkling blue water, and the beautiful sky. Tyler took her hand, and Kelsey touched the gold band on his ring finger.

"Does that bother you?" she asked.

"No. I know you mean well," Tyler replied.

Kelsey smiled at him. "Are you always going to be so agreeable?" she asked.

Tyler laughed. "No. I'm definitely not," he replied. "I'm on my best behavior."

"This is your best behavior?" Kelsey asked in mock surprise.

"This is as good as it gets, Princess," Tyler replied. Kelsey giggled and looked out the window. She felt mixed emotions being back in Vancouver. She knew why Tyler had brought her, since he hadn't been able to bring her before. But the last time she had driven through Vancouver's downtown streets, she had been nursing her broken heart.

"What are you thinking?" Tyler asked.

Kelsey looked at him curiously.

"You were frowning," Tyler explained.

"It's weird being back," Kelsey admitted. "But I'm glad to be here with you," she said, squeezing his hand.

"I wondered about that," Tyler mused, "I was hoping to make better memories here with you."

"I'm sure you can," Kelsey agreed. The car turned, drove a block, then turned again. Kelsey looked out the window. She knew this neighborhood. Kelsey looked out of Tyler's car window. Bob's condo was in this block.

Tyler glanced at her. "I'm sorry," he said softly.

"Tyler, you don't have to apologize," Kelsey said firmly. She turned the ring on Tyler's finger.

"Pull over," Tyler ordered the driver.

"Yes, sir," the driver said in surprise. He turned into the next block and parked. Directly in front of Bob's condo building.

"What are we doing?" Kelsey asked, as Tyler took off his seatbelt. They had barely been in the car for two minutes, so Kelsey knew they weren't staying here.

"We're stopping," Tyler replied. He opened the door. "Come on," he said to Kelsey.

She looked at him in confusion, but took off her seatbelt and followed him out of the car. Tyler stood on the sidewalk, looking at Kelsey. She looked past him, at the building. Suddenly, without warning, tears came to her eyes. Tyler took her into his arms.

"I thought I would never see you again," she whispered into his sleeve. Tears cascaded down her face.

"Kelsey, I'm sorry," Tyler repeated, holding her tightly.

It all came back to her, standing on this street. All the pain. Every bit of it.

Kelsey sobbed as Tyler held her in his arms and stroked her hair.

"Are you better?" Tyler asked Kelsey a few minutes later. She nodded. They were sitting outside of Starbucks, the cool metal of the chair touching her bare leg. An iced green tea latte sat on the table, surrounded by a mass of crumpled-up napkins.

"I don't know what came over me," Kelsey admitted. She wiped a lone tear with the paper napkin she held in her hand.

"That was a difficult time for both of us," Tyler said.

"You managed to go back to Tacoma without breaking down," Kelsey reminded him.

"I guess," Tyler said. "I think I processed it differently than you did. You had it together by the time you got back to Darrow after spring vacation. I was still in shock."

"I think," Kelsey said, looking up at the glass awning with her wet eyes, "I still can't believe that we're married. Being here reminds me how impossible I thought that would be."

"I get that," Tyler said. "But here we are."

Kelsey nodded. She glanced at the building. "Coming to Vancouver was a good choice," she said. "I had to start over without you then, and I get to start over with you now."

Tyler smiled at her.

"Should we start?" he asked. Kelsey picked up her drink and stood up.

"I think we should," she said.

Kelsey's alarm had gone off some time ago, so she wasn't sure how long the ride took, but it wasn't long. The driver had picked them back up, driven through Vancouver's West End, then over the Burrard Street Bridge. A few turns later, and he parked outside of a large fenced-in house facing a large beach.

"Here we are," Tyler said.

"Bed and breakfast?" Kelsey asked, as she got out of the car.

"Our house," Tyler replied.

"Yours and Lisa's?"

"Yours and mine," Tyler corrected.

As Tyler let them into the house, he explained to Kelsey that the Vancouver beach house had been one of the pieces of real estate in the trust that Lisa had given him when he was a teenager. Up until two years ago, it had been leased to a family, but currently it was rented out on a short-time basis to vacationers.

"If you want to start coming up here regularly, we can take it off the rental market," Tyler said, dropping their luggage on the floor next to the front door.

"That's not necessary," Kelsey said, taking a final sip of her latte.

"You can think about it," Tyler replied. Kelsey placed her empty cup on a placemat on the dining room table.

"OK," Kelsey said. "Where's the bedroom?"

Tyler laughed. "Mrs. Olsen. I'm shocked."

Kelsey shrugged. "We're late," she replied.

"Fine," Tyler said. "Come," he said. Kelsey walked over to him, and Tyler pulled her back outside. He scooped her up into his arms, and carried her into the house.

"You're certainly the traditionalist," Kelsey said, as Tyler set her back down. He winked at her.

"I'll show you the bedroom," Tyler said, lifting up their luggage and taking her hand. "I bet we can think of some traditions we can break."

Tyler led Kelsey up to the bedroom, and she smiled in delight. "Mr. and Mrs." pillowcases graced the large bed. Tyler set their bags down as Kelsey lay back on the bed, fully clothed. Tyler reached down and removed her flip-flops. They fell to the floor.

"Do you want a foot massage?" he asked, Kelsey's right foot in his hands. Kelsey shook her head no.

"I want you," she replied. Tyler lowered her foot back onto the bed, and walked around to the side of the bed.

"You have me," he replied, kicking off his own shoes.

"Then I have what I want," Kelsey said. She patted the "Mr." pillow with her hand, and Tyler got onto the bed. Kelsey leaned over and kissed him. Tyler surveyed her with his sparkling brown eyes.

"Are you sure you're OK?" he asked. Kelsey gave him a look, and sighed. Tyler put out his arm and Kelsey placed her head on it.

"My brain won't shut off," Kelsey admitted.

"We have two more days here. And after that, the rest of our lives," Tyler added. "We could go to the beach."

"You don't mind?" Kelsey asked.

"Of course not. I just want you to be happy," Tyler said, running his finger through a strand of Kelsey's hair.

Kelsey nuzzled up against him and closed her eyes. "I am happy," she said.

"Then I have what I want," Tyler replied peacefully.

A while later, the couple headed across the street to the beach. Kelsey looked around thoughtfully.

"I've been here before," she said.

"You've been to Kits beach?" Tyler said in surprise.

"Jess and I had lunch here," Kelsey said. "There's a restaurant," Kelsey turned, and pointed, "over there."

"I should have asked Jess where the two of you had been," Tyler said.

"It's fine," Kelsey said, taking his hand. She didn't want to ruin their honeymoon, but Vancouver was a minefield of sad memories for her. "I'm going to get past it."

"Is there anything I can do?" Tyler asked.

Kelsey shook her head no. "Just be my husband."

"I think I can do that," Tyler said. They walked past the sunbathers and headed close to the edge of the water. Kelsey stopped at the point where the water gently lapped her feet, and Tyler stood behind her, arms around her bare waist, chin on her hair. Kelsey smiled at his touch.

"It's beautiful," Kelsey said as she looked out onto English Bay.

"You're beautiful," Tyler commented.

"When was the last time you were in Vancouver?" Kelsey asked.

Tyler was silent for a moment. "High school," he replied. "No, college. Zach and I stopped by on our way back from Whistler."

"Is Whistler nice?" Kelsey asked. She knew that there was a famous ski resort there, and it had been the home of the Winter Olympics.

"Beautiful. We'll have to go up sometime."

"Do you have a house there?" Kelsey teased.

"No, but Zach's family does," Tyler replied seriously.

"I'm starting to think you're so rich because you never have to pay for a hotel," Kelsey said.

"We're rich, you mean," Tyler replied. "Perhaps you forgot that you became a millionaire on Saturday?"

Kelsey looked up at him, then turned back to the water. She had forgotten. Five million dollars had been transferred to her as part of their pre-nuptial agreement.

"Anyway, my money is your money now," Tyler went on. "And vice-versa."

"I suppose," Kelsey said.

"When will you talk to my financial advisors?" Tyler asked.

"Sometime after we get back," Kelsey said noncommittally.

"The money is there, whether you want to admit it or not," Tyler said.

"Stop annoying me, Tyler," Kelsey snapped. Tyler laughed. Kelsey turned and looked at him. "What's so funny?"

"Now Kelsey has to spend my money," Tyler said.

"No, I don't," Kelsey pouted.

"You promised," Tyler replied.

Kelsey frowned. "I know," she said, in defeat. She had promised Tyler that once they were married, she would spend his money, whether she wanted to or not. It seemed that Tyler would be holding her to that promise.

"Good," Tyler said brightly, "No more fights about money."

"I'll find other things to fight about," Kelsey said sassily.

"That I believe," Tyler replied.

"You don't seem concerned," she commented.

"If we fight, we have to make up."

"So?"

"Making up with each other could be quite fun," Tyler replied. He leaned down and kissed Kelsey's neck with butterfly kisses.

"Tyler, we're in public."

"Kelsey, we're married," Tyler retorted.

Kelsey giggled. She leaned back on him comfortably. "Yes, I guess we are," she said happily.

"It's such a beautiful day, with my beautiful bride," Tyler said to Kelsey. "Should we sit on the beach for a while?"

"For a few minutes," Kelsey teased. "But that's all."

Tyler laughed and took her hand. They walked down the sand. A few paces away they sat at the edge, near the water. Kelsey removed her flip-flops and leaned on Tyler. He put his arm around her.

Kelsey looked out on the water. It was interesting being here with Tyler. She had missed all of this — the beauty, the nature — when she had been here with Jess. It was as if Vancouver had been covered with a gray cloth of emotions before. Now she felt like she could enjoy it, only if her heart would let her. But Kelsey was still finding it difficult.

Places had always held a lot of emotion for Kelsey. Port Townsend was home, but it was also where she had been steps away from ruining her life for good. She could never go there without reminders of what she had been, what she had done. It was part of the reason that Kelsey had wanted to get married there. She wanted to reclaim Port Townsend for herself — and by marrying Tyler there, it was a step in that direction.

Portland, in many ways, was pure bliss for Kelsey. It was where she had been reborn. Her past was behind her, her future in front of her. There was nothing to hide from there.

Kelsey was still trying to decide where Seattle fit in her map of emotions. Darrow had been difficult, but of course, it had also been where she had met Tyler. Simon's office was a mix of pleasure and pain. Virtually every moment she had spent there had been with Tyler, but of course, some of those moments, when Kelsey had thought that they were not meant to be together, still stung.

Now of course, they were here. Vancouver, the place where Kelsey had thought that all was lost. There had been so little good to counteract the bad before now. On her last visit, Kelsey had missed the beautiful beaches, the majestic pine trees. She had missed it all, because her heart missed Tyler. Now she was here again, with him. Together.

But Vancouver had been the place where she had lost all hope. Part of her wanted to cry just thinking about how desperately sad she had been, despite the fact that she was here with Tyler now. It would take time for her to heal, and that made her sad too.

Kelsey watched as a seagull swooped down from the sky, towards the blue water. Kelsey felt all of this sadness, and she was having trouble shaking it off. She didn't want to talk about it with Tyler, for fear that he would feel guilty for bringing her here now. After all, he was the one who had sent her up with Jessica, so many months ago.

Kelsey wondered what it was that made place so emotional for her.

Was it like that for everyone?

Kelsey wondered if Tyler felt the same about the places he had been. She looked at him, and he looked back at her and smiled. Kelsey leaned her head against his shoulder and looked back out onto the water. She would try again with Vancouver. She had to. Kelsey would reclaim Vancouver from the sadness and make it the place where she and Tyler got their start. It would be the place that Kelsey would always remember fondly, with love.

She just needed to find a way to forget the sadness.

The sun streamed down on them as people enjoyed the beach around them. Kelsey loved moments like this with Tyler, but she had discovered something else that she enjoyed doing with him.

"Should be go back in?" she asked him.

A while later, Kelsey lay in bed, attempting to catch her breath. The bed sheets had been tossed to the floor, and they lay in a pile next to Kelsey's navy-blue bikini. Tyler lay next to Kelsey, breathless as well.

"You are amazing," Tyler said to her.

Kelsey smiled, then took a deep breath. "The feeling is mutual, Mr. Olsen," she managed to say.

Tyler slipped his hand around her waist and kissed her shoulder. "Now what?" Tyler asked.

"I'm tired," Kelsey said, snuggling against him.

"Me, too. But I'm hungry. My bride is starving me."

"You have better things to do than eat," Kelsey said, unapologetically.

"Well, that's true," Tyler agreed. "However, I need to keep up my strength."

"You should work out more. I'm fine," Kelsey teased.

"Yes, it does turn out that my bride has quite a bit of stamina."

Kelsey giggled. "So does my husband," she said seductively. "OK, you can have something to eat. What should we get? Should we order out?"

"I feel like I should take you out. It is our honeymoon."

"All the more reason to stay in," Kelsey said. She stroked his bare chest with her hand.

"You've talked me into it. Do you care what we get?"

"No. Do you mind if I take a nap until it comes?"

"No," Tyler said. He stood up and picked up the sheets. He gently lay them over Kelsey, bent down, and gave her a kiss. "Get some sleep. I'll wake you when it's here."

"OK," Kelsey said. She closed her eyes as Tyler walked out of the room.

Kelsey woke up to Tyler stroking her hair as he sat next to her on the bed.

"Hungry?" he asked. "The food's here."

Kelsey yawned. "OK," she said sleepily. "I'll be right down."

"I could bring it up to you," Tyler said.

"That's all right. I can't stay in bed forever," Kelsey said.

"OK," Tyler said, kissing her cheek. He stood up and left the room. Kelsey yawned again, and tossed the sheets off her naked body. She looked around, spotted her bag by the door, and walked over to it. She reached in and pulled out her black satin robe, the one she had received at her bridal shower. Kelsey slipped it on, tied the belt, and left the bedroom.

The house was really cute. Kelsey hadn't taken the time to explore it, but just from what she had seen, it was a perfect beach cottage. A really large beach cottage. She walked down the stairs and over to the living room. Tyler had laid out an Indian feast.

"Wow," Kelsey said, sitting down.

"I was hungry," Tyler said, turning to her. A sexy grin came over his face. "Wow," he said.

"We were about to eat," Kelsey commented.

"Exactly what I had in mind," Tyler replied.

"I bet," Kelsey said. She picked up a spoon from one of the dishes. "Yum. This looks great, Tyler."

"You look great, Kelsey," Tyler replied.

"Thank you. So do you. But we're going to eat dinner now," Kelsey said, picking up her plate and putting rice on it.

"I thought you weren't that hungry," Tyler commented.

"That was before I saw the food," Kelsey replied. She picked up the bowl of *channa masala*, and put some on her plate. Tyler gave her a smile, and got a plate of his own.

"Are you sure you don't want me to take you anywhere?" Tyler commented as they ate.

Kelsey looked up from her plate of food, which was delicious. "I don't need to go anywhere," she replied.

"Don't you want to see Vancouver?"

"I can see Vancouver anytime," Kelsey replied.

Tyler surveyed her with his chocolate-brown eyes.

"Still reveling in the pleasures of your groom's body?" he asked.

Kelsey grinned. "Yes. Is that a problem?"

"Not with me, it isn't," Tyler assured her.

"Good," Kelsey said. "We can come up one weekend and look around. We have other things to do this week."

"Do we?" Tyler teased.

Kelsey looked at him sharply. "You bet we do," she replied, taking a bite of food.

After dinner, Kelsey got dressed, and they walked across the street to the beach. They spent a few minutes looking at the water, then they began walking on the path back toward the Burrard Bridge.

Kelsey looked at Tyler in the evening sun. His chestnut-colored hair shone in the sunlight.

"Do you feel different about us?" Tyler asked her.

Kelsey thought for a moment before answering. "Not yet," she said honestly. "Do you?"

"A little," Tyler admitted.

"Is that good or bad?" Kelsey asked.

"It's good," Tyler said. "I feel a responsibility to you."

"How is that different than before?" Kelsey asked. Throughout their relationship, Tyler had always shown a lot of concern for her.

"I guess I feel that now that a lot of my family drama is over, that I need to work hard at building my family with you," Tyler said.

"Is your family drama over?" Kelsey asked in surprise. "I guess Chris was pretty nice to Lisa in his speech," she mused.

"Chris was nice to Lisa in his speech because she had just given him two hundred million dollars," Tyler scoffed.

"She did what?" Kelsey said in disbelief.

"The day we got married, Lisa and Chris signed a settlement agreement. Lisa created a trust that Chris and I are the beneficiaries of, but since I won't be taking any money out of it, it's effectively Chris's."

"And the trust is for two hundred million dollars?" Kelsey asked.

Tyler nodded yes. "Chris agreed that he wouldn't touch the principal, but it will make at least ten million in interest a year. Probably a lot more."

"So Lisa's paying Chris ten million dollars a year not to sue her again?"

"Actually, she's paying him ten million dollars a year not to depose me again," Tyler said. "Lisa would be perfectly happy to keep fighting him in court."

Kelsey considered this. "She really cares about you," she commented.

"I know. I guess I feel like she's finally starting to understand that if she cares about me, she has to care about the people that I care about. Including you."

"I see that," Kelsey said.

Tyler bit his lip and looked at Kelsey. "Do you think you can forgive her?" he asked.

"What do you mean?" Kelsey asked.

"When you were crying...," and Tyler paused for a moment, "it was because of what Lisa did to us."

"It was," Kelsey admitted. She sighed. "I don't know, Tyler. I guess I'm not really upset, I mean Lisa's been really generous to us, and it seems like she's trying to make amends. I think I'm just still on edge. She's difficult to predict, and I'm not sure if she likes me. Lisa could just be pretending, because she doesn't want to upset you."

"I suppose you have a point," Tyler said.

"I'm trying to put my bad feelings aside," Kelsey said, "I know that the reason that she attacked me is because she loves you. And I suspect that she won't attack again because she loves you, and now she understands how important we are to each other." Kelsey took a deep breath. "But in the back of my mind, I worry that if there's ever a moment when we aren't getting along, or if she thinks I'm not good for you any more, I'll be a target again. And that stops me from feeling completely safe."

"There's really nothing I can do, is there?" Tyler said.

"No," Kelsey admitted.

"I want the two of you to get along. I think that Lisa would like you if she took the time to get to know you."

"I want that too. Tyler, we'll have plenty of time to get to know each other."

"Chris's speech really made me think," Tyler said as the path curved east. "Neither of my parents know anything about you because they are always wrapped up in their own lives."

"Isn't that true for you too? They don't really know you either," Kelsey pointed out.

"I guess you have a point."

"You are their son. And whatever meaning they attach to that relationship, that's how they will deal with you. Now, I'm their daughter-in-law. It's going to be the same. They probably will never know the real me, because they aren't the type of people to care. It's like my mom — for her I'll always be fourteen. She is so sure that she understands who I am, that she's never bothered to question her belief."

"I get that, but at least Kelly knows something about you, even though it's flawed. Jeffrey knows more about me than Lisa, despite the fact that I don't tell him anything."

"True, but Tyler, your mother isn't just your mom. She's in charge of a multi-billion-dollar company that spans the globe. No matter what you want, she's never going to be focused on you."

Tyler looked at Kelsey, a look of realization on his face.

"That's what's wrong, isn't it? That I can't ever have a parent devoted to caring just about me."

"Maybe. I know that's something you probably always wanted, but your parents just aren't like that."

"But you are. You care about me," Tyler said, and Kelsey smiled at him.

"I do. And you care about me too."

"So maybe it doesn't matter about them."

"I don't think it does. You and me and Lisa and Chris, we'll all get along when we have dinner, or when we go visit them during the holidays. But the relationship that matters is you and me. And I'm confident that one is going to work out fine."

Tyler kissed Kelsey's hand. "I am too."

Kelsey hugged Tyler's arm, and her blonde hair blew in the breeze.

"I guess that's what's bothering me," Tyler continued. "I want to have a real family relationship with you, but I don't know what that looks like. I'm afraid that I'll go back to work and I'll forget what's important."

"You won't. You aren't like them. You care about relationships. And that includes your relationship with me."

"I think that they care about relationships too, but everything is seen through the lens of what's important to them. They never consider anyone else's perspective."

"But you do."

"Sometimes. I can be selfish."

Kelsey laughed. "Everyone can, Tyler."

"I'm really worried about this, Kels."

"Why? You aren't going to turn into Lisa."

"I wonder if Lisa was always like this, or if the situation that she found herself in made her the way that she is."

"What do you mean?"

"Being CEO. Having no time to think about anything but getting through your schedule the next day." Tyler paused, then continued. "Chris — I think he's just self-absorbed, and I'm starting to understand that, but I feel like Lisa has changed."

"Maybe, but why do you think so?" Kelsey asked curiously.

"I don't know. Seeing her with Bill Simon, maybe. Or when we were at dinner with Chris. It's like they see a different Lisa than I'm used to."

"Different how?"

"More loving. Less cutthroat. I don't know. They just seem to relate to her differently than I do."

"Maybe it's just because they picked her to be in a relationship with," Kelsey hypothesized.

"Maybe," Tyler smiled at Kelsey. "We're supposed to be on our honeymoon, and we're talking about my parents."

"That's OK. A honeymoon is about beginning to build a family together. We'll have to see what each of us brings to the relationship, and that includes our family baggage."

"You don't have any," Tyler commented.

"I do. I don't understand my mother," Kelsey replied.

"You don't think so?"

Kelsey shook her head. "No. I don't think I ever will."

"Jeffrey said that he really enjoyed working with her."

"Jeffrey was being nice," Kelsey commented.

"Jeffrey isn't nice when he doesn't get along with someone," Tyler replied.

"Interesting," Kelsey said. "What are you afraid of, Tyler?"

"Hurting you. Being so wrapped up in my own concerns that I don't realize that you're in pain."

"I think that's really unlikely."

"I have a lot of baggage, Kelsey."

"No, you have a lot of responsibilities. I've known you for a long time, and not once has there been a moment when I felt like you didn't care about me. What frightens me is that I worry that there will be times when you don't care about you."

"I know," Tyler said.

"That's what I want you to focus on. I can take care of myself."

"I want to take care of you," Tyler replied.

"We can take care of each other," Kelsey said firmly. "Look, our families are crazy. However, they love us, and we love them. But you and I are going to build our own family, and we're going to do it our own way. We don't have to follow their rule book."

"I know you're right," Tyler said.

"I married you knowing that you're going to be the CEO of Tactec one day. You married me knowing that I want to make partner. Our careers will have to co-exist with our relationship. Lisa might not have figured out how to do it, but you will. I'm going to tell you if I need more, and you're going to do the same, and we're going to make our love last."

Tyler smiled. "You promise?"

"I do," Kelsey said. "Don't worry so much. I love you."

"I love you too, Princess. I just always want you to know that."

"I always do," Kelsey replied.

They were in sight of the Burrard Marina, and Kelsey saw lots of beautiful sailboats bobbing up and down on the water.

"Should we turn back or keep going?" Tyler asked. "I think we're almost out of path."

"We can turn back," Kelsey said. They paused for a moment to look at the water, which was sparkling in the fading summer sun, then they headed back toward Kitsilano Beach.

"What do you want from our marriage?" Tyler asked.

"To be loved," Kelsey replied.

"Is that all?" Tyler asked curiously.

"I don't know," Kelsey admitted. "I was really excited to get married, because I love you."

"I love you too."

"I'm glad," Kelsey said. "I'm not sure that I know what marriage means.

It seems to mean such different things to people, and I'm not sure that I have my own definition yet."

"What do you mean by that?" Tyler asked.

"Well, to Jess, marriage means having children, and building a family that way. Of course she loves Ryan, but I think both of them would have been dissatisfied if they hadn't started with kids. Bob, on the other hand, for him marriage seems to be an outward demonstration of his internal feelings. He wants to show the world he's successful, so he marries a socialite. He wants to show the world he's a family man, so he marries a woman with four kids. And for your mom, I think it means being in love. I think that's why she hasn't gotten re-married."

"That was interesting at the dinner with Lisa and Chris," Tyler said. "I don't think I realized that she had truly been in love with Chris until then. I assumed that she had gotten married because of me."

Kelsey nodded. At dinner, she had heard Lisa's pain from when Chris left her, and it had surprised Kelsey.

"I just don't know what marriage means to me yet," Kelsey continued. "I think that maybe I'm like your mom, and it means being in love, but a part of me knows that I would have been just as in love if you never asked me to marry you. I don't think you would have been, though. But for me, I'm just happy to be with you."

"What do you think marriage means to me then?" Tyler asked.

"I think that's for you to decide," Kelsey replied.

"I know, but what do you think?"

Kelsey was thoughtful. "I think it means stability. I think you crave a normal life, and although you realize that you're not ever going to have that, you're going to try to make any area of your life that you do have control over as peaceful as possible." Kelsey gave him a smile. "That's why I'm wondering why you chose to marry me." she teased.

Tyler laughed. "I think you're right," he mused. "About all of your theories. Why did you agree to marry me if you didn't care about getting married?"

"Because I knew it was important to you," Kelsey said. "And of course, I can sleep with you now."

Tyler laughed again. "You could have slept with me before. No one but you and Jess would have cared."

"I know," Kelsey said. "But I'm actually glad I waited."

"I'm glad the waiting is over," Tyler stated.

"Me, too," Kelsey agreed.

"I wonder," Tyler began, "if the reason Bob won't marry Morgan is because the right symbolism isn't there. Maybe he feels like he's showing the stereotype of the older man with the younger wife to the world, and he doesn't want to do that."

"Possibly," Kelsey said.

"He sure doesn't want to give her up, though," Tyler said.

"Yeah," Kelsey agreed. That was clear from Bob's behavior at the wedding. Kelsey had noticed something else at the wedding, and she had a question for Tyler.

"Zach's interested in Morgan, isn't he?" she asked.

"Morgan needs to stay away from Zach," Tyler said flatly.

"That's not an answer," Kelsey replied.

"I don't care who Zachary is interested in, because he doesn't get a vote in who he's going to end up with," Tyler replied.

"That's a fair point."

"The last thing I want is Zach to break someone else's heart because they aren't good enough for the Payne family," Tyler continued.

Kelsey agreed. With her Associate degree, it wasn't likely that Morgan would get past Mrs. Payne's academic screening, particularly since Mrs. Payne had a Ph.D..

"Does Morgan like Zach?" Tyler asked.

"She thinks he's cute," Kelsey said.

"I'm glad she's in San Francisco then," Tyler said.

"That doesn't seem to be stopping Bob," Kelsey commented.

"So I've heard," Tyler said.

"But Ryan doesn't know."

"No. I hope it stays that way."

"I do too. He's going to be pretty busy soon, so maybe it doesn't matter," Kelsey said.

"Maybe. But I think Ryan always has time to meddle in Bob's private life."

"That's probably true," Kelsey agreed. "I guess Jess and Ryan have moved into their new house next to Lisa."

"I told you," Tyler commented.

"I know. I didn't want to believe you," Kelsey said.

"Brace yourself. If we have kids, the pressure is going to be on to move into the compound as well."

"I don't want to have kids for a long time," Kelsey said.

"Works for me," Tyler replied.

"You'll be a great father, though," Kelsey added.

"I'm going to work on being a great husband for now," Tyler replied.

Kelsey smiled at him. "I think you already are," she said.

Kelsey lay in bed a while later, and took a very deep breath. She was hot, her heart was pounding, but she was totally, utterly relaxed. Tyler walked back into the room. Naked.

"Hi, there," he said, lying in bed next to her. He kissed her on the lips.

"Hi, yourself," Kelsey said, snuggling into his arms. She was blissful.

Tyler sighed happily.

"I hope every night is like this," he said.

"We have to go to work sometime," Kelsey replied. She closed her eyes and cuddled him. Tyler smelled wonderful.

"Don't remind me."

"I won't," Kelsey said. They only had tonight and tomorrow — then she had to go back to work herself. "Are we going back to Seattle tomorrow?"

"I thought we'd just drive down on Wednesday morning, and I can take you straight to the office."

"That's time out of bed," Kelsey teased.

"I know. But we aren't taking the yacht back," Tyler said.

Kelsey opened her eyes and looked at him in surprise. "Why? Is Bob using it?"

"There was a message on my phone when we got back from our walk," Tyler said. A phone had been waiting in the house when they arrived. Tyler would leave it behind in Canada. "Bob fired the entire crew of the yacht."

"No. Why?" she asked.

Tyler hesitated for a moment, then he said, "Because someone on the yacht told Ryan that Morgan was there with Bob."

"Morgan was on the yacht with Bob when?" Kelsey asked. Tyler was being a little vague.

"The night of our wedding. Morgan took the yacht back to Seattle with Bob."

Kelsey looked at Tyler and waited. She knew there was more.

"She stayed in his room. With him," Tyler said.

"Oh, boy," Kelsey said, leaning back on Tyler's arm. "Who told you?"

"Everyone. Ryan told me about Bob, Jeffrey told me about the crew."

"Maybe we should stay here," Kelsey said, burrowing her face into Tyler's pillow.

"I could transfer to the Vancouver office," Tyler commented.

"I don't even know what to think," Kelsey said.

"Morgan's an adult," Tyler replied.

"I know," Kelsey said.

"I didn't mean to ruin your night," Tyler said.

"You didn't," Kelsey said, cuddling against Tyler again. "It's nice to be here with you. I need to stay out of Morgan's private life, but it's just difficult for me to do that."

"She's your friend."

"Yeah," Kelsey said. Tyler stroked Kelsey's face. "My family really, just like Ryan and Bob are yours. What did Ryan say?"

"Nothing surprising. I told him to focus on Jessica and the babies, since Morgan's back in San Francisco."

"She didn't stay?"

"No," Tyler said. "Jeffrey told me," he commented.

"There are really no secrets," Kelsey said.

"It comes with the money," Tyler replied. "Too many people, with too much time on their hands not to gossip."

"So I guess everyone knows that I'm not letting you leave our bed," Kelsey said.

"Actually I'm the person telling everyone that bit of information," Tyler teased. Kelsey laughed. "Want some covers?" Tyler asked.

"Sure," Kelsey said. Tyler reached down and pulled a soft cotton sheet from off the floor. He arranged it over her.

"We don't seem to like bedding," Kelsey noted.

"It gets in the way," Tyler said. "Anyway, it's not cold."

"Not yet," Kelsey said, closing her eyes and cuddling against Tyler. She rubbed her feet against his.

"So will we spend the day in bed again tomorrow?" Tyler teased.

"I let you leave the house today."

"For an hour?"

"Hour and a half," Kelsey corrected. "Count your blessings."

"I do. One of them is in my arms," Tyler said, kissing her hair.

"You're so romantic," Kelsey said.

"I try," Tyler said. "Are you tired?"

"A little. You wear me out."

"We can sleep."

"Only if I can stay in your arms," Kelsey replied, suppressing a yawn.

"Please do," Tyler said, pulling her closer.

The next morning, Kelsey put her hair into a ponytail.

"Are you ready?" she asked Tyler.

"Ready," Tyler said, walking out of the en-suite bathroom. He, like Kelsey, was dressed to go running. Kelsey took his hand and led him out of the bedroom and down the stairs. Tyler picked up a set of keys which were hanging by the door, and they left the house. Outside, their town car was waiting. Tyler let Kelsey into the car, then he walked around and got into the other side.

"Let's go," Tyler said after they put their seat belts on. The chauffeur complied, and the car pulled away from the curb. Tyler took Kelsey's hand.

The town car drove back through Kitsilano, and over the Burrard Bridge. They turned on Pacific Avenue, and Kelsey looked out of the window in interest.

"I didn't see this part of Vancouver last time," she commented as they drove through a busy commercial area.

"I'm not sure I've been here either," Tyler said.

"How many times have you been to Vancouver?" Kelsey asked.

"More than I can count. Lisa liked to come up for hockey games when I was a kid," Tyler replied.

"Hockey? Lisa likes hockey?"

"Lisa loves hockey," Tyler replied. "She grew up watching it in Minnesota."

"Does she play?"

"Definitely not. But she's an avid watcher."

"That's surprising to me."

"Lisa's full of surprises," Tyler replied.

"I hope not," Kelsey teased.

Tyler laughed. "Good ones from now on, Princess," he said.

The town car pulled up next to the Starbucks on Denman Street and Kelsey opened her door.

"We'll call you when we're ready to go back," Tyler said to the driver.

"Yes, sir," the driver said as Tyler got out. He joined Kelsey on the sidewalk.

"Isn't it pretty?" Kelsey asked, looking out onto English Bay.

"She's very pretty," Tyler said, putting his arm around Kelsey's waist and giving her a kiss.

"Come on," Kelsey said, taking Tyler's hand and heading across the street.

After stretching on English Bay Beach, Kelsey and Tyler ran, following the seawall route around Stanley Park. For Kelsey, the run was particularly cathartic. The last time she had been in Vancouver, she had run this exact same route twice, alone and mostly in tears.

"Look," Kelsey said, pointing at the marina as they reached the end of the run. "Isn't that where we got off the yacht?" She looked around at the scenery around them.

"I think so," Tyler replied. They had slowed to a walk and were once again holding hands.

"Is Bob's yacht still there?" Kelsey asked.

"No. He fired the crew when they returned to Seattle," Tyler replied. "You know, if you want to take the yacht back, Jeffrey can arrange for a different crew."

"Driving is fine," Kelsey said.

"Are you sure?"

"I can manage to control myself for a couple of hours. Anyway, I have to go to work. I'm going to need to get used to not being in bed with you."

"I can't believe you need to go back to work tomorrow," Tyler said. "Simon is such a pain."

Kelsey didn't say anything. She knew that Tyler had dozens of reasons to dislike Bill Simon, and the fact that Kelsey needed to go back to work in the middle of the week was only one of them.

"I'll enjoy today with you," Tyler said, kissing her hand.

"Good. Are we heading back home?" Kelsey asked hopefully.

"Not yet," Tyler replied.

"Really?"

"Really. Don't be so impatient, Mrs. Olsen."

"Fine," Kelsey pouted.

They walked out of the park and into Vancouver's West End. Kelsey had been on this street before. It was the one Bob's condo was on.

"Where are we going?" Kelsey asked as they crossed Bute Street.

"Bob's condo," Tyler said.

"What? Why?" Kelsey asked. She didn't particularly want to break into tears again.

"Because you need to have better memories here," Tyler said. "We'll probably stay here in the future, and I don't want you to be sad then."

"So I should be sad now."

"You won't be sad," Tyler said firmly, pulling her into the building.

Kelsey was quiet as they walked across the lobby and went up the elevator. She was trying to suppress her emotions. Tyler had a point, but she still didn't want to be here. They walked off of the elevator, and Tyler opened the door of the condo. Kelsey hesitated at the doorway.

Tyler looked at her. "Come in," he said, gently pulling her.

Kelsey took a deep breath as she looked around. It was exactly the same as before, when she had been here with Jess. The same elegant design, the same luxurious feel. It had been wasted on her before. Before, when she had been an emotional wreck.

Tyler closed the door.

"Which room was yours?" he asked. Kelsey looked at Tyler, curiously. "Show me," he said firmly.

"Fine," Kelsey said. She walked into the room she had stayed in. The room she had cried herself to sleep in. Kelsey took another deep breath. She felt so uncomfortable here. She couldn't wait to leave.

Tyler looked around in interest. Then he sat on the bed.

"What are you doing?" Kelsey asked. "I want to go," she said, turning away from him.

"Kelsey," Tyler called to her. Kelsey turned back to him. Tyler was taking off his shirt.

"What?" Kelsey said. She was irritated.

Tyler smiled.

"Take off your clothes," he replied.

Kelsey looked at Tyler in surprise.

"You must be kidding," she said flatly.

"You need a better memory here," Tyler said. "I'm going to give you one."

Kelsey looked at Tyler in disbelief. Every fiber of her being wanted to leave this room, wanted to leave those terrible memories behind. And here Tyler was, wanting her to stay.

"I can't," Kelsey said softly.

"You can," Tyler replied. He smiled at her. "You know you want me," he added.

Kelsey bit her lip. Tyler certainly had that right. She couldn't have managed to resist him if she had tried over the past few days. And she wasn't sure she could now. But her emotions were in freefall.

"Is it too much?" Tyler asked curiously. Kelsey nodded yes. Perhaps Tyler wouldn't press her if he realized how much emotion she was feeling. Tyler stood up and took her hands. He kissed her, hard.

"Too bad," he said. "You have to get past this. I won't let you be afraid of an empty room," Tyler said firmly.

Kelsey looked around. She could feel tears forming in her eyes, but she blinked them away.

"OK," Kelsey whispered. She knew Tyler was right. Now she just needed to convince herself.

"OK," Tyler said with a smile. He led her to the bed, and they lay down next to each other on the soft pillows. Kelsey wondered if they were still full of her tears.

Tyler put his arm around her and Kelsey turned toward him and buried her face in his bare chest. Tyler stroked her hair gently.

"Tell me something good about this room," Tyler said.

"There is nothing good about this room," Kelsey replied, her voice muffled.

"Come on. There must be something. Think."

"Why are you doing this?" Kelsey snapped.

"Because you're stronger than this," Tyler replied, unapologetically.

Kelsey frowned. "You always think you're right, Tyler Olsen," she said.

"I'm right about you. Kelsey doesn't let anything or anyone defeat her."

"I know," Kelsey said. And she did. Tyler continued to stroke her hair. "OK, in this room I realized that I no longer had control of the world. Sometimes I would have to accept that things wouldn't always go my way just because I wanted them to."

"That's a valuable lesson," Tyler said.

"Great, can we go now?" Kelsey said.

"I told you, you need a better memory here," Tyler replied.

Kelsey bit her lip unhappily. She sat up and took off her tank top. "Then get to it," she said.

"Get to it?" Tyler laughed. "This isn't about sex, Kelsey."

"No? Then what's it about?" Kelsey demanded.

"It's about acceptance."

"What do you mean?"

"You need to accept that bad things happened to you, that it wasn't fair, but that you moved on."

"I have accepted that," Kelsey said grumpily.

"No, you haven't."

"Yes, I have. That's your problem, not mine."

"What do you mean?" Tyler asked curiously.

"You and Chris. And Lisa," Kelsey said. "You haven't accepted what they've done to you." Kelsey had more to say, but she stopped herself. Because she could tell from Tyler's expression that she had struck a nerve.

"You're right," Tyler said thoughtfully. "But this isn't about me now. I'm not Kelsey. I'm not the warrior princess."

Kelsey laughed at the reference. "I'm not the warrior princess either."

"You are," Tyler said firmly. "That's why we're here. I need you to be strong."

"I can't be strong about this," Kelsey said quickly. "I always fail when it comes to emotions."

"Not this time," Tyler replied. "This time you're going to win."

"I don't know what you want from me here," Kelsey said. "What do you want me to say?"

"I want you to forgive Lisa," he said. "I want us to go back to Seattle, and for you to have put all of this, everything behind you."

"Why?" Kelsey asked.

"Because I want you to show me how it's done," Tyler said simply.

"What do you mean?" Kelsey asked.

"I know that it's important to you for me to try to get along with my family," Tyler said. "That's why we went to Gig Harbor to see your grandparents, so you could prove a point. But I have no idea how to get started. I engineered a truce that cost my mother two hundred million dollars, but there's no amount of money that she can give me to buy my forgiveness."

"OK," Kelsey said, not quite understanding.

"If you can forgive her, then I'll have a blueprint to use so I can forgive her. But that can't happen if you haven't processed what happened here, in Vancouver."

Kelsey considered what Tyler was saying. He had a point. Vancouver was where Kelsey had done most of her healing. When she had returned to Seattle she had a lot to do, and focused on doing it. In Vancouver, she had had nothing but time.

"OK, I understand," Kelsey said. She lay on Tyler's arm. "In this room," she said softly, "I thought about how much I loved you."

"Did you?" Tyler asked, and Kelsey heard the smile in his voice.

"I did," she said, and it was a happy memory. "I thought about how much I trusted you, and how despite the chaos, I knew that believing in you was the right thing to do."

Tyler turned to her, and kissed her forehead.

"I remember being here," Kelsey said thoughtfully. "And I was looking at the ceiling, and it was blurry because I had cried so much, and I thought to myself how grateful that I was that I had had you in my life, because you taught me what it was like to feel loved. I knew that even if I never had that experience again, that I would always remember it, and feel it in my heart. No one would ever be able to take that away from me." Kelsey glanced at Tyler. "And now here we are."

"Yes."

Kelsey reached out and stroked his face. "I love you so much. That's what I learned in this room."

Tyler smiled at her. "And now you have a good memory in this room," he said.

"I do," Kelsey agreed.

Tyler sat up in bed and reached for his shirt.

"Hey, what are you doing?" Kelsey asked.

"What?" Tyler said, holding his shirt in his hand.

Kelsey gave him a look. "I thought we were going to bed."

Tyler shook his head. "I didn't say that," he replied.

Kelsey pouted, and Tyler laughed.

"Oh, is that what you thought we were here for?" he teased.

"Come here, you," Kelsey said, as she pushed Tyler, who was laughing, back down on the bed.

"So, where should we eat in this neighborhood?" Tyler asked. Once again, the bed was stripped of its sheets and clothes were scattered on the floor.

"No idea," Kelsey said.

"You were here for a week," Tyler said.

"We mostly went to the grocery store downstairs and bought food there," Kelsey replied.

"That's unfortunate. I was hoping that you would have a recommendation," Tyler said. He picked up his phone. "What are you in the mood for?"

"Anything."

"There's a nice Northwestern cuisine restaurant a few blocks from here," Tyler said.

"Do they deliver?" Kelsey asked.

"What do you mean?" Tyler asked.

"Tyler, we ran here. Perhaps you forgot," Kelsey said.

Tyler smiled. "I suppose I did," Tyler said. He reached for his phone. "That's what the concierge is for," he commented.

Forty-five minutes later, Kelsey was sitting on the sofa in the living room, wrapped in a white terry-cloth robe. Her running clothes and Tyler's were in the washing machine. The doorbell rang and Tyler stood up to answer it. Tyler gently ran his hand across the back of Kelsey's neck as he passed by her, and Kelsey smiled at his touch.

Tyler opened the door, and said "Thank you." Kelsey heard the door shut, and she looked over at Tyler eagerly. Then she frowned.

"What's that?" she asked. Instead of a restaurant bag, Tyler had a garment bag draped over his arm.

"Clothes," Tyler replied.

Kelsey looked at Tyler, completely puzzled.

"Clothes? You had the concierge buy us clothes?"

"I thought you wanted lunch," Tyler replied, as he set the bag in a chair, and unzipped it. He pulled out a blue oxford-cloth shirt.

Kelsey opened her mouth and closed it. She had no idea what to say.

"Here," Tyler said, removing a blue-and-white sundress from the bag. "This is for you."

A few minutes later, Kelsey and Tyler were walking down Georgia Street, holding hands. Kelsey's sundress fit her perfectly and matched with the new royal-blue lace-up espadrilles on her feet. Tyler was business casual in his blue shirt and khaki pants. Dark-brown boat shoes completed his look.

"Did it occur to you that we could have just ordered food?" Kelsey asked. She was still a little stunned.

Tyler shrugged. "I didn't want it to get cold."

"Tyler, we're walking to the restaurant. It wouldn't get cold in the few minutes it would have taken to deliver it."

"Do you mind eating out with me, Kelsey?" Tyler asked.

"I guess not," Kelsey said.

"Good," Tyler said as they turned on Howe Street.

Moments later, the couple walked into the restaurant and were seated.

Kelsey was thoughtful as she looked at the menu.

"Do you know what you want?" Tyler asked. "I think I'm going to get the steak."

Kelsey peered at him from behind the menu.

"Yes, Mrs. Olsen?" Tyler asked brightly.

"That was an extravagance that I'm not used to," Kelsey said.

"We've bought clothes to eat in before," Tyler pointed out.

Kelsey thought back. She supposed they had.

"I feel like that was different. Jess and I were trying not to ruin the designer clothes we were wearing," she said.

"And today, we didn't have clothes to wear."

"Sure we did. Back in the house."

"The house is across the bay."

"Tyler, it's ten minutes away," Kelsey replied.

"And ten minutes back to the restaurant. What difference does it make? You look pretty."

"That's not the point," Kelsey said.

"What is the point?" Tyler asked.

"The point is that it was an unnecessary expense."

"Have you not met Jeffrey? Almost everything he spends my money on is an unnecessary expense," Tyler replied.

Kelsey laughed. She supposed Tyler had a point.

"Look, you said that once we got married, you wouldn't complain when I spent money on you. I just spent money on you, so no complaining."

"I'm not complaining. I'm just pointing it out."

"It sounds like complaining," Tyler said. "I don't see the big deal. It's a pretty dress. You can wear it again."

"I guess," Kelsey said.

"Just decide what you want to order, Mrs. Olsen," Tyler said. "And don't pick the cheapest thing."

Kelsey frowned.

After lunch, Tyler and Kelsey strolled around downtown. Their gold wedding rings gleamed in the summer sun. Kelsey had given her engagement ring to Jessica for safekeeping after the wedding, not knowing where Tyler was taking her. She hadn't wanted to lose it on a campground, or misplace it in a luxury hotel.

"Did you say that you were planning on driving me directly to work tomorrow?" Kelsey asked.

"I thought we'd get up early, have breakfast, and drive straight to Simon's office," Tyler verified.

"We can't," Kelsey said in disappointment.

"Why not?" Tyler asked.

"I didn't bring my work clothes to Canada," Kelsey replied. "I'll have to drop by home first."

"That's out of the question," Tyler replied. "Unless you can go in late. I don't want you to have to get up at 4 a.m."

"You mean you don't want to get up at 4 a.m.," Kelsey commented.

"That too. Buy something here."

Kelsey glared at Tyler. "We just bought something here," she pointed out.

"Buy something else. I'm not getting up before 7."

Kelsey raised an eyebrow, and Tyler gave her a sexy grin.

"I mean I'm not getting out of bed before 7," he clarified.

"Tyler, I don't want to go shopping," Kelsey said.

"Fine. Don't go shopping. I'll have the concierge at the condo buy something for you. They can deliver it to the house," Tyler said as he pulled out his phone.

Kelsey put her hand on the phone. "Stop. Fine. I'll get something for myself." They were a few feet away from a mall, and Kelsey didn't really want to send the concierge out for a second time when all she needed was a dress and a pair of shoes.

"OK," Tyler said, putting his phone back into his pocket. "Should we look here?" he asked, gesturing to the mall.

"Let's go," Kelsey said.

The couple walked into the mall, which was flooded with natural light. Kelsey glanced around.

"Over there," she said, pointing at a designer boutique. One of the things

Kelsey had noticed about Vancouver on her last trip was that although Canada was a different country, they had many of the same brands she was used to in Seattle. It meant that this shopping trip could be quick.

Kelsey led Tyler into the Vancouver branch of an American designer. Kelsey had bought several work dresses from their Seattle store, so she was confident she could find something to wear.

"I'll just be a minute," Kelsey said.

"Take your time," Tyler replied, leaning against a glass counter. "Let me know if you need any help trying things on." Kelsey glanced at him, and he gave her a seductive smile.

"I'm sure I can manage," Kelsey said, turning to the racks.

A few minutes later, and Kelsey had in her hands a pretty shirtdress that would look great both in and out of the office.

"It looked really nice on you," Tyler said, as Kelsey left the dressing room, back in her sundress.

"Thanks. I'll get it," she said, about to pull out the tiny wallet she carried when she went running.

"You mean I'll get it," Tyler corrected.

Kelsey frowned.

"Tyler, I can easily afford this dress," Kelsey said, and it was true. She made a good salary at Simon and Associates, and had virtually no expenses.

"What did we agree, Kelsey?" Tyler asked.

Kelsey frowned in defeat. "Fine," she said, holding the dress out to him.

"This is one of the reasons that you need to go talk to my financial advisors," Tyler said, Kelsey's dress in a bag in his hand. "They can give you access to your accounts."

"What do you mean my accounts?"

"Just like Jess, you'll have ATM and debit cards," Tyler said. "If you'd prefer, Jeffrey can bring them to you, but I thought that you would want to know the overall portfolio first."

"Tyler, I really don't need to know about your money," Kelsey said, as they walked into a large department store for shoes.

"Really, Kels?" Tyler said.

"Why is it so important to you?" she asked.

"It's a kind of big part of my life, Kelsey," Tyler replied.

"It doesn't define you."

"Of course it does. It defines you too."

"What do you mean?" Kelsey asked.

"You know what I mean, Kelsey," Tyler replied.

Kelsey frowned. She did know what it meant, but a part of her still wanted to pretend that she and Tyler, and their relationship together, were completely ordinary.

"I'll talk to them later," Kelsey said. "It's not like I've had time."

"I know, but you don't even know how much money you have under your own control," Tyler pointed out. "So I'm a little concerned that you're going to put off knowing how much I have."

"How do you know that I don't know about my own money?" Kelsey asked hotly. She couldn't imagine that Papa Jefferson would have said anything to Tyler. They had a client-accountant relationship, and Papa had a duty to be silent.

"Dan told me," Tyler replied.

"Why?" Kelsey said, perplexed.

"It was one of the few pieces of advice he gave me when we were in Port Townsend. He told me not to let you stick your head in the sand and keep ignoring your financial situation."

Kelsey frowned. "I know how much money I make at Simon's. And I use it wisely. I don't need to keep track of all of the other extras."

"Kelsey, you have about five and a half million dollars worth of 'extras'," Tyler commented. "So maybe you should pay just a little attention to them.

"I don't need a lecture from you," Kelsey said, as they walked into the women's shoe department. "Mr. Moneybags," she added testily.

"You can't hide forever, Kelsey," Tyler replied, unconcernedly. "The money's there whether you pay attention to it or not."

"Then I don't need to pay attention to it," Kelsey said, picking up a pretty blue shoe.

"Kelsey," Tyler said in exasperation.

Kelsey glanced at him. "Be quiet, and let me spend your money," she replied.

A while later, Kelsey and Tyler were strolling through Yaletown. They had returned to Bob's condo, picked up their dry running clothes, and left them — along with Kelsey's new work clothes — with the concierge. Their driver would pick them up and deliver them to the beach house later.

"So I considered taking you over to Grouse Mountain, but somehow I have a feeling that you've been there too," Tyler said as they walked on the sidewalk and passed stylish boutiques.

"I have," Kelsey said. "Bob recommended that Jess and I go."

"Of course. Bob," Tyler said. "I'm really dreading going back. Maybe I need to go back to work on Wednesday too."

"Why?" Kelsey asked. Because of Tactec's generous vacation policy, Tyler had planned on taking the rest of the week off, returning to work the following Monday.

"Well, I told Ryan that since I had some time off, I'd go over and help them get ready for the twins, but now the only thing Ryan's going to be talking about is Morgan."

"Sorry," Kelsey said, squeezing his hand.

"It's certainly not your fault," Tyler said. "It's been nice being away from the drama."

Kelsey hugged his arm. "It's been nice being with you." She smiled up at him. "My husband."

Tyler grinned. "I love when you call me that."

"It's true. We've been married for almost 72 hours."

"How has it been so far?" Tyler asked. "I'm taking a survey."

"We could be in bed more, but so far, so good," Kelsey replied. Tyler laughed, and Kelsey gave him a grin.

"You're a lot of fun," Tyler said.

"Thanks. So are you," Kelsey replied.

"Are you looking forward to going back?" Tyler asked. "Settling in?"

Kelsey shrugged. "I've lived at Ryan's before, so I can't imagine that it will be so different. Except I won't have my own room this time."

"You can," Tyler teased.

"I think not," Kelsey replied. She beamed at him. It was so nice to be with Tyler, and to be his wife. She was still trying to wrap her mind about what that meant, and to understand how she felt, because she had so many different feelings right now.

Of course there was the intimacy. That was definitely a plus. And she was having a really good time being with Tyler. Slowly she was beginning to love Vancouver, and to get past the emotions of her previous visit.

But there was the money.

Kelsey had resolved that she would just have fun on the honeymoon, and let Tyler do what Tyler loved to do, which was spoil Kelsey. And it had been fine for a while.

Until it wasn't.

It wasn't the first time that Tyler had bought an outfit that Kelsey *could* wear to work, but it was the first time that he had specifically bought one *for* it. And It felt weird. Kelsey went to work and made her own money, but now, as Mrs. Tyler Olsen, she couldn't spend that money on a work dress.

As the perfect summer sun shone on the couple, Kelsey felt her inner turmoil. She knew it would come up, but it had returned so quickly. She hadn't even managed to walk into their new home yet, and already, her discomfort over Tyler's money had returned. And the thought of going to Tyler's financial advisors and having them unveil the reality of Tyler's assets. It was almost too much to bear.

She glanced at Tyler, who looked blissfully happy. Kelsey wanted to feel that way, to feel that sense of inner peace. She thought that she could get there one day, that the time would come when Tyler's money felt like her money too, just as Tyler wanted it to be. But as she held Tyler's hand, she knew today would not be that day.

"Should we go to the park?" Tyler asked her.

"Sure," Kelsey said.

Tyler surveyed Kelsey. "I'm feeling like Vancouver was a particularly bad choice for our honeymoon," he commented.

"No. I'm happy to be here with you," Kelsey said quickly. Of course Tyler would pick up on her mood.

"Then what's wrong?" Tyler asked.

Kelsey gave him a smile. "Nothing a ride on the swings won't cure," Kelsey replied.

A ride on the swings, and an hour later, Kelsey and Tyler were sitting by the sparkling water. Kelsey sat barefoot in the green grass, Tyler's head in her lap. She absentmindedly ran her fingers through his hair.

"Do you remember being in Gramercy Park?" Tyler asked her.

"Of course," Kelsey said.

"I dreamed of being with you like this then," Tyler said.

"You should have told me," Kelsey said.

"So you could have run away?" Tyler teased.

"I don't think I would have run away," Kelsey said. "I liked you already."

"You did not."

"I did too," Kelsey said.

"Really?" Tyler said in surprise.

"Really," Kelsey replied, leaning down and giving him a kiss.

"I was such an idiot," Tyler commented.

"You were just cautious."

"You really liked me then?" Tyler said.

"Why don't you believe that? I danced with you, remember?"

"I remember that quite vividly," Tyler replied.

"See. Now you know," Kelsey said, stroking Tyler's hair.

"You have no idea how happy you've made me," Tyler said.

"The feeling is mutual, Mr. Olsen," Kelsey replied, kissing him again.

Kelsey held Tyler's hand as the fading summer sun streamed into the bedroom that evening. She ran her finger leisurely across his wedding ring and Tyler kissed her bare shoulder.

"We should come back up here," Kelsey said.

"Whenever you want to, Princess," Tyler replied.

"It won't be for a while," Kelsey said.

"I know," he said flatly. Tyler knew as well as Kelsey did that between her work and his, the birth of the Perkins twins, and the Tactec summer party, they wouldn't be likely to have another free weekend soon.

"It doesn't matter. Like Bill Simon said, every day will be a holiday with your bride."

Tyler laughed.

"Right. Bill Simon's been divorced twice. He doesn't know anything about romance."

Kelsey smiled. She wondered if Tyler's mother would agree with her son's sentiments. But of course, there was no way Kelsey was about to ask. It was risky enough to mention Bill's name these days. She turned toward Tyler, and he gently put his arms around her.

"Is there anything else you want to do before we leave?" Tyler asked.

"Be with you," Kelsey replied, kissing Tyler on the lips. "How about you?"

"I'm exactly where I want to be," Tyler replied, stroking Kelsey's back.

"I wonder how many hours we've spent in bed," Kelsey mused.

"We needed to make up for lost time," Tyler said.

Kelsey giggled. "I'm glad that everyone knows not to ask 'what did you do on your honeymoon.'"

"Maybe your friends don't," Tyler said. "Ryan's going to ask for a full report." Tyler saw the look in Kelsey's eyes. "He won't get it," he added.

"Good. He doesn't need to know," Kelsey said, snuggling up to Tyler's bare chest.

"Ryan's always curious about things that don't concern him," Tyler commented.

"True," Kelsey agreed.

"I'm really hoping that the twins manage to distract him."

"I doubt it. Ryan and Jess are going to have a lot of help, so they won't be busy," Kelsey said.

"True." Tyler looked thoughtful. "It's funny. After dinner with Chris, I'm curious to talk to Cherie."

Kelsey looked at Tyler in surprise. "Really? Why?"

"She broke up two marriages," Tyler replied. "She must be an interesting person."

"Interesting?" Kelsey said. She thought for a moment. "Well, Jess thought that she was very nice."

"That's another thing. Everyone uses the word 'nice' when they talk about her. Bob, Jess. Even Lisa. Yet Ryan hates her. So that's interesting too."

"When is she coming?" Kelsey asked.

"When Jess is in labor. Bob's plane is in New York for Jess's mom, and he's got a private plane in Miami on standby for Cherie."

"Miami? I thought Cherie lived in Palm Beach?" Kelsey said, as she stroked Tyler's chest.

"The Secret Service has been shutting down the airport and the roads constantly lately. Cherie didn't want to be stuck in Palm Beach, so she's staying in a hotel in Miami."

"I wonder what Ryan's going to do while she's here?" Kelsey asked.

"Whine. Pout. Usual Ryan behavior."

Kelsey giggled. "You're lucky that you sort of get along with your parents."

"Sort of."

"OK, you don't hate your parents," Kelsey clarified.

"I'll go along with that one," Tyler said.

"Does Ryan know about Chris and Cherie?" Kelsey asked. She just realized that maybe that was a reason for Ryan's feelings.

"According to Lisa, Bob doesn't even know about Chris and Cherie. So I don't know how Ryan would have found out."

Kelsey looked at Tyler with wide eyes. "Wait, how does Bob not know?"

"Cherie didn't tell him."

"Lisa didn't either?" Kelsey said in disbelief.

"Bob honestly believes that Cherie left because she thought that he was having an affair with Lisa," Tyler said. "At least that's what Lisa says."

"Why didn't Lisa tell him the truth?" Kelsey asked.

"Bob and Cherie were having a civilized divorce, and she didn't want Ryan to get hurt," Tyler said.

"How do you know all of this?" Kelsey asked.

"Lisa and I talked before she signed the paperwork for Chris's trust," Tyler replied.

"That's amazing," Kelsey said. "That's a really big secret to keep."

"Lisa said that she figured Bob would figure it out on his own once Chris and Cherie got married, but they never did."

"Wow," Kelsey said. "You aren't going to tell Ryan, right?"

"No way. I'm not going to feed Ryan's conspiracy theories," Tyler replied. He stroked Kelsey's hair with his hand.

"Now I'm interested in meeting Cherie," Kelsey said.

"Told you," Tyler said. "I'm sure you'll have plenty of time to talk. I bet one of our jobs when the babies are born is to keep Cherie away from Ryan."

"How long will she stay in Seattle?" Kelsey asked.

"I don't know. She doesn't work, so it's not like she needs to hurry back to the East Coast."

"Is she staying in a hotel?"

"Bob's house."

"Are you kidding me?" Kelsey said.

"Bob gets along with her," Tyler shrugged.

"Bob gets along with everyone," Kelsey mused.

"Most people would think that's a good thing, Mrs. Olsen," Tyler commented.

"I'm just worried about Morgan," Kelsey admitted.

"I know," Tyler said, caressing her. "But she's back in San Francisco, and Bob will be busy with the twins."

"Yeah," Kelsey said, unappeased.

"You can't solve everyone's problems," Tyler said wisely.

"I know. I can't even solve my own."

"What problems do you have?" Tyler asked, with a bit of surprise.

Kelsey looked into Tyler's chocolate-brown eyes. They were full of concern. She smiled.

"I'm looking at him," she teased.

Tyler leaned over and kissed her passionately.

Kelsey looked around the bedroom, making sure that she hadn't forgotten anything. She smiled at the thought that there was no need to look anywhere else in the house. Although she had spent two nights here, she still didn't know what most of the rooms looked like. She made a mental note to explore the next time they stayed.

"Ready, Kels?" Tyler asked, as he walked into the room.

"I'm ready," she said.

Tyler set his phone on the dresser. "Then let's go," he said, scooping both of their bags into his hand. He used his other hand to take Kelsey's hand into his own, and they walked out of the bedroom and out of the house.

A rental car was parked outside on the street. Tyler opened the car door for Kelsey, then opened the trunk and tossed the bags in. He joined Kelsey in the front and turned on the engine.

"How did this car get here?" Kelsey asked as she put on her seat belt.

"It was delivered this morning," Tyler replied.

Kelsey looked at Tyler. She marveled at the fact that it meant nothing to him that a car had been dropped off in front of his million-dollar beachfront residence so he could drive to his new four-million-dollar residence.

"You didn't want the Porsche?" Kelsey teased.

"Jeffrey offered to bring it up, but I told him it wasn't necessary," Tyler said, as he pulled away from the curb.

Kelsey looked at Tyler in disbelief as they turned the corner.

"You have no idea how privileged you are, do you?" she asked him.

Tyler glanced at her, then put his eyes back on the road.

"Of course I do. You're my wife," he replied with a smile.

A little over two hours later, Kelsey stood in the lobby of her office building, looking at Tyler.

"I'm going to miss you," he said, running his hand over her sleeve.

"I'm going to miss you too, but I'll see you soon," she said.

"What do you want me to bring for dinner?" he asked.

"Anything," Kelsey replied. At some point, she wanted to start having dinner at home with Tyler, but since it was her first day back, she knew it wouldn't be tonight.

"OK," Tyler said, leaning over and kissing her. "I'll be by at seven."

"All right. Say 'hi' to Ryan," she replied. She reached over and stroked his face. Tyler sighed unhappily and gave her another kiss. "I'll see you soon," Kelsey said. She gave him a wink and walked over to the elevator bank. She pushed the up button, but a second later, she felt Tyler's arms around her.

"Tyler," she scolded.

"Tell Simon you quit, and come back to bed with me," Tyler whispered in her ear.

"Stop tempting me," Kelsey said. The elevator door opened, and Kelsey turned and gave Tyler a quick kiss. "I'll see you at seven," she said as she stepped on the elevator and pressed the button to her floor.

"Bye, Kelsey," Tyler said, looking at her unhappily.

Kelsey blew him a kiss as the elevator doors closed. She felt a little sad as the elevator rose. She knew that she would miss Tyler today. Their honeymoon had been blissful, and Kelsey hadn't wanted it to end. However, she knew, just as Tyler did, that even though she was now Mrs. Tyler Olsen, that wouldn't be enough for her. She wanted to be as successful in work as she felt that she was in love.

Kelsey walked into the doors of Simon and Associates. Tori ran past her.

"Hey, welcome back!" Tori said, turning her head back.

"Thanks," Kelsey said with a smile. Clearly the office hadn't changed while she was gone.

"Hi, Kelsey," Millie said as Kelsey reached the front desk. She handed Kelsey a large stack of mail.

"Hi," Kelsey said. "This is all mine?" she said in concern.

"Afraid so," Marie said.

"Your wedding was amazing," Millie gushed.

"It was. We had so much fun," Marie agreed. "Wait until you see our pictures."

"I'll look forward to it," Kelsey said.

"The summer associates are in a meeting with Bill," Marie said. "You can meet them once they're done."

"OK," Kelsey said, glancing through the stack and heading towards her office. "Has anyone quit yet?" she asked.

"They just started on Monday," Millie said.

"So expect someone to quit tomorrow," Marie quipped. Kelsey giggled and walked on.

"Stop!" Jake called just as Kelsey walked in front of his office.

"Why?" Kelsey asked, looking up from a CLE flyer.

"Don't look at your desk yet," Jake said quickly, jumping out of his chair and running out to Kelsey.

"Why not?" Kelsey asked curiously. Jake took her arm and steered her back to the reception desk.

"Let me introduce you to the summer associates first," Jake said firmly.

"I thought they were in a meeting," Kelsey said, as they walked past Marie and Millie, who had gone back to their work.

"It will just take a minute," Jake replied. He and Kelsey walked to the large conference room, where Bill Simon and five summer associates sat. "Kelsey's back," Jake said as they entered the room.

Everyone looked up at her.

"Hi," Kelsey said uncomfortably, but Bill Simon smiled at her.

"Welcome back, Kelsey. Kelsey is our second Intellectual Property attorney. Jake, do we have time for everyone to introduce themselves?"

Kelsey looked at Jake quizzically. *What was Bill talking about?*

"I think so," Jake said firmly.

"OK," Bill said with a smile. "Tiana, why don't you start?"

A pretty and petite African-American with goddess braids looked at Kelsey, who was still holding her pile of mail.

"I'm Tiana Reid, second year from the Richardson School of Law, University of Hawaii," she said brightly.

Once the students were done introducing themselves, Kelsey wandered back over to her side of the office, passing the empty reception desk on her way.

Kelsey heard, "Surprise!" She looked up from the legal newsletter she was reading, and gazed into her office. A smile crossed her face.

"You guys," she said happily.

A few minutes later, Kelsey and everyone else in the office was standing around the conference room outside of Kelsey's office, eating a catered breakfast. Kelsey's actual office was decorated with cream-and-navy balloons. A pile of gifts sat on her client table, and to Kelsey's amusement, a pile of work sat on her desk. But next to the work was a vase of cream-colored flowers — which Tyler had sent — and on the door was Kelsey's favorite gift, a nameplate that now read, 'Kelsey Olsen'.

"We had so much fun," Millie said. She was scrolling through the photos on her phone. Everyone from the office had taken the cruise ship from Seattle and back, and from the photos, it was clear that everyone had a really good time. Kelsey had seen photos of Jake in the kiddy swimming pool with his wife and baby, Marie playing basketball with her two teenage boys, and a short video of Bill Simon singing a duet with Lisa Olsen at karaoke.

"He can't sing," Marie said sadly, making Millie laugh.

At the party, Kelsey discovered that Tiana and a first-year from UPenn named Dirk had been assigned as the summer associates for the Intellectual Property department. Tori and Raj were already taking bets on how long the summer associates would last.

"Great odds for anyone betting that any summer associate stays the whole summer," Tori said with a wink.

"That's really depressing," Kelsey commented to Jake after the party. No one in the office expected that any of the summer associates would still be around by the time that the new permanent associates arrived in August.

"Maybe we could talk one of them into staying. We could make a killing," Jake mused.

"Jake," Kelsey scolded.

"Don't judge. I didn't just marry a billionaire," Jake replied.

Kelsey laughed. "You have a point, though," Kelsey mused. "They always leave so quickly. Maybe we could figure out why and help them stay."

"Kelsey. We know why. Bill Simon's crazy."

"I know," Kelsey said, and she mentally scolded herself for agreeing, "but we managed to stay. Why?"

"I'm desperate," Jake shrugged.

"That's not it. You've been here for almost a year. You could walk out of the door and get hired by anyone now."

"Good point. Maybe it's time to update my resume," Jake said thoughtfully.

Kelsey frowned. "Look, it's going to look terrible on their resumes when they put 'Simon and Associates, one week.' Let's help someone."

"What's the point?" Jake asked.

"Well, if it's the IP summer associate, you and I could take entire weekends off. We'd have a lot of help."

"OK," Jake said, warming to the idea. "We can try."

"Great," Kelsey said. She was determined.

"So how much should I put you down for?" Jake asked.

"What do you mean?" Kelsey asked, confused.

"Of course you're going to bet too?"

"Jake."

Jake lifted an eyebrow.

"Fine. Ten bucks," Kelsey said with a sigh.

Tori and Raj accepted Kelsey and Jake's ten-dollar bets, with the agreement that the summer associates couldn't know about the betting pool, so there would be no side deals. Kelsey took the very last date in the summer associate calendar, while Jake, who was less confident in their persuasion skills, took a date two weeks earlier. Everyone else in the office, including Bill Simon, had selected dates in July.

After eating lunch at her desk and messaging Tyler, who was at the Bellevue branch of Target with Ryan, Kelsey pushed her work aside and began to strategize. She and Jake had decided that they would focus their efforts on Tiana, the second-year IP summer associate. First and foremost, the longer Tiana stayed, the less work the duo would have to do, and the more work they could drop on her desk. Second, they thought that a second-year summer associate would feel as though they would have more to lose by leaving early.

Kelsey pondered why she and the other associates who were still there had stayed. She knew that for her, Bill had been a really great mentor, and because of that, she hadn't considered leaving, even though she now had opportunities to do so. From talking to Tori, she knew that Tori was having a similar experience. Both of them had been given responsibilities that only senior attorneys would have at larger firms. Kelsey had not only represented Tyler, but had also led the discovery team in Arizona. As for Tori, Bill had rotated the M&A team so every member had the opportunity to be lead attorney.

Kelsey discounted Tyler's experience, as she felt that he had been mostly avoiding Tactec. However, even Tyler felt as though he had learned a lot at Simon and Associates. Kelsey thought for a moment, then she stood up and walked over to Jake's office in her slippers.

"Hey," Jake said, looking up from his sandwich.

"Why are you still here?" Kelsey asked.

Jake looked at her quizzically. "Because I work here," he replied. "Unless Bill has fired me, in which case, I'll go."

Kelsey smiled. "Sorry. What I meant is, why haven't you left along with everyone else?"

"I told you, I'm desperate."

"Seriously, Jake," Kelsey said.

Jake put his sandwich on the wrapper and thought for a moment.

"Actually, I considered it pretty seriously around the time we went to Arizona. Bill didn't seem to like my work much, and I was a little concerned about how long I was going to last. But Tyler suggested to me that if I told Bill that I was serious about trying to improve my work, that he would give me a chance. I think it also helped that you were working on Tyler's proxy fight, and that Tyler was leaving. I was the only person left in IP, so Bill might have been less inclined to fire me too. When you and Tyler were in New York, Bill spent some time talking to me about how I could improve, and I took his advice."

"Why do you think Devin is still here?' Kelsey asked.

"I think that Devin really likes being the senior attorney at the firm."

"Really?"

"Devin's really into status," Jake said. Kelsey didn't know Devin well enough to know. He was a little standoffish, and Kelsey had never made a real effort to get to know him. She had plenty of other things to do at Simon and Associates.

"That's helpful," Kelsey said.

Jake smiled. "You really want to win the bet," he teased.

"It's a challenge," Kelsey said.

"Do you have a plan?" Jake asked.

Kelsey leaned against the doorway. "Maybe," she replied. "I think that our summer associate needs a mentor."

"Interesting. Is that the reason that you think people leave?"

"I'm starting to think so. Because so many people show up at once, I bet that they feel like they are thrown into the deep end of the pool, so the easy thing to do is quit. But if they had a little individual attention, maybe they would stick around."

"So you're going to mentor Tiana?"

"We are," Kelsey replied.

Jake looked doubtful. "I have a lot of work, Kelsey," he said.

Kelsey put her hands on her hips. "We're doing this together," she replied.

"It was your idea," Jake said.

"Jake," Kelsey warned.

"OK, Kelsey, what do you want me to do?" Jake asked.

"I'll let you know," Kelsey replied.

"I expect a cut of the profits if I help you win," Jake said, picking up his sandwich.

"You wanted to see me, Mrs. Olsen?"

It took Kelsey a moment to realize that Tiana was talking to her. Kelsey wasn't used to being called Mrs. Olsen by anyone but Tyler.

"Kelsey. Please come in, Tiana," Kelsey said, gesturing to a client chair. Kelsey looked at Tiana, who looked a little nervous. Kelsey remembered being just like her. A summer associate, the first week in a new internship, terrified that she was about to screw up. Kelsey gave her a bright smile.

"I just wanted to have a chance to meet you," Kelsey said. "We'll be working together all summer," she continued, optimistically, "and I wanted to find out a little bit about you."

"Oh, OK," Tiana said.

"So are you from Hawaii?" Kelsey asked.

Tiana nodded. "Honolulu."

"Where did you work last summer?" Kelsey asked.

"A local firm. Brown and Horowitz."

"So how did you happen to come to Seattle?"

"Well, Seattle has a reputation for having the most cutting-edge technology companies, and I think I'd like to work in IP."

"Why Seattle instead of Silicon Valley?"

"Seattle seemed a little more livable than California," Tiana said.

Kelsey could tell that she was feeling a bit more relaxed. "I've heard that too," she agreed.

"Where are you from?" Tiana asked.

"I'm from a small town on the Olympic Peninsula," Kelsey said.

"Did you go to the University of Washington for law school?" Tiana asked.

"No, I went to Darrow," Kelsey replied.

"Darrow? Really?" Tiana said. And just like that, Tiana was nervous again. Kelsey supposed that some people found the idea of Darrow Law School quite intimidating. Kelsey decided to change the subject.

"So," she said smoothly, "I was wondering what you were interested in learning over the summer. Did you have any types of projects that you particularly wanted to work on?"

Tiana shook her head no. Kelsey wasn't surprised. Most law students didn't have any idea what actually went on in a law firm. She hadn't.

"I do a lot of licensing work," Kelsey said. "So if you're interested in that, I'd be happy to teach you what I know."

Tiana beamed. "That would be great. There's a Licensing Intellectual Property class that I wanted to take in the fall, and I've been kind of nervous about it."

"Well, I'd be happy to help," Kelsey replied with a smile.

"Princess," Tyler said from Kelsey's doorway later that night.

"Tyler!" Kelsey shouted. She jumped up and dashed across the room and into Tyler's arms.

"I missed you," Tyler said, hugging her.

"Me, too," Kelsey admitted. She had been busy all day, but Tyler's kisses were always at the top of her mind.

Tyler tipped Kelsey's face up and kissed her passionately. Kelsey thought she would melt in Tyler's arms as his lips caressed hers.

"I'm at work," Kelsey protested weakly as Tyler kissed her neck.

"Come home with me," Tyler replied, nuzzling her.

"Working," Kelsey breathed.

"You know you want to play," Tyler said, running his hand over her back.

Kelsey certainly did. After a day deprived of Tyler, her body burned for him.

"Soon," Kelsey managed to say, and she disentangled herself from his arms. But she made the mistake of looking into his sexy brown eyes, and her insides fluttered with desire.

Tyler smiled at her knowingly. "Are you sure?" he asked.

Kelsey wasn't sure at all, but she managed to nod yes.

Tyler surveyed her once more, then put a bag on her desk.

"If I can't convince you to leave, I suppose we'll have to eat dinner here," he commented.

"Thanks, Tyler," Kelsey said. She took a deep breath and looked inside the bag to distract herself from Tyler's body. "Margaret made lasagna?" she asked. Kelsey reached inside the bag and took out a large tray.

"She knows you like it," Tyler said, sitting in a client chair.

"She sent over so much," Kelsey said, pulling out a large foil-wrapped half-loaf of cheese bread.

"Margaret asked me why I was so hungry today when I was in the kitchen," Tyler said. Kelsey glanced at him, and he grinned.

"Did you tell her that your bride starved you during the honeymoon?" Kelsey teased.

"I told her I spent too much time in bed to get up and eat," Tyler replied.

"You didn't," Kelsey pouted. Tyler shrugged. Kelsey frowned and pulled out a fabric bag of utensils. She handed Tyler a fork. "Eat all you want now," she commented.

"I'd rather have something else," Tyler said, licking the empty fork. Kelsey felt herself go scarlet.

After a few bites of Margaret's delicious lasagna, Kelsey sat in the client chair next to Tyler and balanced her bare legs across his lap. Tyler set his fork down onto the client table, next to the pile of presents, and stroked her leg with his hand.

"How was your first day back, Princess?" Tyler asked.

"Busy," Kelsey said. "The summer associates are here."

"How much did you bet?" Tyler asked.

Kelsey giggled. "Ten dollars," she replied.

"Who's running the pool this year?"

"Tori and Raj. Aren't you supposed to ask me what date I picked?" Kelsey asked.

"As long as it's in July, you've got as good of a chance as anyone," Tyler replied.

"I picked August 31st," Kelsey replied, leaning over and taking another piece of lasagna with her fork.

Tyler looked at Kelsey quizzically.

"So you want to lose?" he asked.

"I'm going to win," Kelsey said firmly.

"Not by betting that at least one summer associate is going to stay through August, you aren't," Tyler replied.

"I have a plan. Anyway, you stayed all summer. Twice."

"I had a reason to stay," Tyler said. "I was avoiding Lisa."

"Well, Jake and I are going to make sure that the IP summer associate has a reason to stay too," Kelsey replied.

"Are you going to tie him up and lock him in a closet?" Tyler teased.

"Her. And no, that's not the plan," Kelsey sullenly.

"OK," Tyler laughed. He reached out and took a slice of cheese bread. "What is?"

"I think that summer associates leave because they don't have a mentor. We're going to change that this year."

"That's an interesting theory," Tyler said. "Being here in the summer does feel a lot like trying to find a lifeboat for yourself."

"Exactly. Jake and I are going to solve that for Tiana."

"And let everyone else drown? Simon's hired at least four summer associates, right?"

"Can't save everyone," Kelsey said with a shrug, eating the lasagna on her fork. She looked at Tyler. "Who won your years?" she asked.

"Christine won the first year I was here," Tyler said, "And the second year, I was excluded from the pool of contestants, since they knew I'd be around. Marie won that year."

"I didn't realize that Simon would bet," Kelsey said.

"He's going to be working against you," Tyler said, taking another piece of lasagna.

"No, he's not," Kelsey said dismissively, breaking off a piece of cheese bread for herself.

"Don't kid yourself, Mrs. Olsen. Bill Simon only hires summer associates so he has warm bodies around when the regular associates want to take vacation. He couldn't care less if they stay."

"You think?" Kelsey said in surprise.

"Bill's probably taken July 15th in the pool," Tyler replied.

Kelsey laughed. "That's so cynical, Tyler," she said.

"But true. Ask him," Tyler said, eating.

"I can't. Then he'd know what we were up to."

"We? You mean you. Jake's not going to do anything."

"Jake picked August 10th, so he's probably going to do something."

"Jake probably figures that you'll do enough work to keep her here past August 1st. Then it's smooth sailing for him," Tyler replied.

"Again, very cynical."

"I'm just calling them as I see them, my love," Tyler said. He leaned over and took a bite of the cheese bread in Kelsey's hands.

"I think we can do it," Kelsey said, ignoring Tyler's comment. "Worst case, I'm out ten bucks."

"What will you do if you win?" Tyler asked.

"Take my husband out to dinner, of course," Kelsey said smiling at him. Tyler looked at her with his sexy brown eyes.

"Actually," Tyler said softly, reaching out to stroke Kelsey's hair. "I think I'd rather have dessert."

After dinner, Kelsey went back to her work, while Tyler surfed on his phone and waited for her.

Around ten, Bill Simon looked in. "Mr. Olsen, I didn't know that you were in the office," he commented.

"Kelsey's here," Tyler replied.

"We're happy to have her back," Bill Simon said, giving Kelsey a smile. "How's Tactec?"

"Tolerable," Tyler replied.

"Glad to hear it. Kelsey, are you done with Romano?"

"Almost. I'll send it to you before I leave," Kelsey replied as she typed.

"Thanks. I'm heading out, so tomorrow morning is fine," Bill said, turning to leave.

"Hot date?" Tyler asked, surprising Kelsey.

Bill Simon looked at Tyler curiously. "Tyler, I've been friends with your mother for decades," Bill commented. "Far longer, in fact, than she ever even started thinking about you."

"Interesting," Tyler replied thoughtfully. "I suspect that Keiko Payne would say the same about you, Mr. Simon."

Kelsey noted the uncomfortable look on Bill Simon's face, but he spoke.

"Indeed she might, Tyler. Have a good night, you two," Bill said, and he left the room.

"What was that about?" Kelsey asked Tyler.

"What?" Tyler asked innocently.

"Tyler," Kelsey warned.

"Finish up. We'll talk about it later," Tyler replied.

Kelsey stretched and closed her laptop an hour later.

"Ready?" Tyler asked.

"I am. Thanks for waiting for me."

"Where else would I be?" Tyler asked.

"You don't have to bring me dinner every night," Kelsey replied, walking over to him. Tyler placed his hands around her waist and leaned his head on her tummy.

"I want to when I can, because there will probably be nights that I can't," Tyler replied. Kelsey stroked Tyler's chestnut brown hair, and he looked up at her.

"Let's go home," he said.

Kelsey smiled at him. "OK," she said.

A short car ride and dozens of kisses later, Tyler carried Kelsey over the threshold of their new home, Ryan's old condo.

"Oh, wow!" Kelsey said, as Tyler set her down gently in the living room. Once again, the condo had been transformed.

"Do you like it?" Tyler asked. Kelsey looked around in amazement. Instead of the bright colors that Jessica preferred, now the condo reflected the warm, muted colors of nature that were Kelsey's favorites. She felt like she was back on the Pacific coast, in the forests of Kalaloch.

"I love it," she said honestly. "Thank you." She put her arms around Tyler.

"You're welcome." Tyler said, kissing her. Kelsey looked up into his chocolate eyes. She stroked his face with her hand and felt her heart speed up.

"Show me the bedroom," she whispered.

"Yes, Mrs. Olsen," Tyler replied, taking Kelsey into his arms once more.

Kelsey groggily turned off her alarm the next morning. Tyler's arms were around her naked body and she looked over at him.

"Good morning, Princess," he said without opening his eyes.

"Hi," Kelsey said, kissing his nose. Tyler reached out and pulled Kelsey to himself for another kiss.

"Going to work?" he asked.

"Yes," Kelsey replied. She was slowly waking up.

"Do you want me to go with you?"

"No," Kelsey replied. Even when Tyler went back to work at Tactec, he would almost never need to get up as early as Kelsey normally did. She gave him another kiss, wriggled out of his sleepy grasp, and got out of bed. She walked over to the en-suite bathroom, put on one of the terry-cloth robes hanging there, and left the bedroom.

She had been too distracted last night to explore, so as the sun shone over Elliot Bay, Kelsey wandered out into the living room. This would be their new home, and she wondered what other changes had been made while they were away. She walked into the bedroom that had previously been Jessica's dressing room, and discovered that it had been turned into a luxurious library/study. There was plenty of room for both her and Tyler to work in the room together, and the thought made Kelsey smile. She loved being with him, and it was nice to have a place where they could work together, since she knew that they would both have plenty of work to do. Kelsey walked back through the living room. Except for the colors, the living/dining room/kitchen hadn't changed dramatically from when the Perkins couple lived there, and that was fine with Kelsey. She didn't expect that she would be using any of those areas differently than she had during her previous stays.

Kelsey peeked into Tyler's former room, which was now a cozy family room, with a large screen television. Then she walked next door, and saw that Jessica's former room was unchanged, a comfortable ivory-colored guest room. Kelsey frowned as she turned back to the living room. She had thought that there would be a treadmill in the condo.

Kelsey looked back into the family room, but there was no exercise equipment there. She was surprised. Jeffrey knew how important working out was to Kelsey, and every other place that she had lived had a gym on site. But she knew from living here previously, that there was no gym in this building. It was why she had worked out in the gym across from Collins Nicol, and Tyler had gone to the Washington Athletic Club. Kelsey had just assumed that Jeffrey would take one of the three extra bedrooms and create a gym that she and Tyler could share.

She stood in the living room, hands on hips, thinking. If there wasn't a gym in the house, that meant that she would have to get up even earlier so she could work out at Tactec headquarters, as she had been for the past few months. Kelsey turned and walked back into the bedroom, where Tyler was stirring.

"Hey," she said, sitting on the bed, and stroking his forehead. "Why don't we have a treadmill?"

"Ryan," Tyler said in explanation. "There's a strict noise covenant that Bob had to agree to so he could buy the apartment."

"Oh," Kelsey said in disappointment.

"Sorry, Princess," Tyler said.

"It's fine," Kelsey said, giving him a gentle kiss. "I'll work out at Tactec."

"OK," Tyler said, closing his eyes once more. Kelsey gave him another kiss on the cheek, then stood up. She walked over to the closet and picked out her work clothes. She had got up too late to work out at the gym today.

A half-hour later, Kelsey was showered, dressed, and ready for work. Tyler was fast asleep again, and Kelsey didn't want to wake him. She closed the bedroom door, put on her shoes, then bit her lip in confusion.

How am I supposed to get to work?

For months, Kelsey had walked to work, usually with Jade. Kelsey glanced at the clock on her phone. It was 7 a.m., which meant that Kelsey was supposed to be escorted by a bodyguard. Kelsey sent Jade a message.

Hi, Jade. Am I supposed to meet you this morning?

I'm outside your door. Jade replied.

Kelsey breathed a sigh of relief. At least one thing was the same. She opened the front door. Jade was leaning on the wall outside of the condo.

"Hi, Kelsey," Jade said.

"Hi, sorry, I have no idea what I'm supposed to be doing this morning," Kelsey admitted, letting Jade into the condo and closing the door behind her.

"It's fine," Jade said. "Welcome back."

"Thanks," Kelsey said.

"Are you ready to go?" Jade asked.

"I am, but did you drive?" Kelsey asked. Jade looked at her curiously.

"Tyler's always driven me to work when we lived here," Kelsey explained.

"I drove my motorcycle," Jade said with a grin. Kelsey thought. Of course, she finally realized. She owned a car. Tyler's BMW, which he had given to her when he took Ryan's Porsche. But Kelsey had no idea where it was.

"Do you know where my car is?" Kelsey asked Jade. Jade gave her another curious look. "The BMW? I haven't driven it in months," Kelsey explained.

"Hang on," Jade said, tapping her phone. "It's in the garage at Simon and Associates," she reported.

"Maybe we should call a taxi," Kelsey said in defeat.

"Take Tyler's car this one time. I can drive it back," Jade said.

"Great idea," Kelsey said. "Let me ask him." She left Jade in the living room and returned to the bedroom.

"Tyler," Kelsey said softly. Tyler turned at the sound of her voice. "Can I borrow your car?" she asked.

Kelsey sat at her desk at Simon and Associates, sipping a large hot mocha from Starbucks. It was her second day back in Seattle, but she felt completely lost. Kelsey had put a sticky note on her desk to remind herself to drive the BMW home in the evening, so she would have a ride in the morning. She also set her alarm an hour and a half earlier, so she could work out at Tactec. Kelsey realized that she wouldn't be getting a lot of sleep now that she was married, and it wasn't just because Tyler would be keeping her awake at night.

Kelsey didn't want to be ungrateful. Most Seattleites would be thrilled to live downtown, and to have access to the excellent gym at Tactec. And

Kelsey had been —when she worked at Collins Nicol and wasn't expected at work until 9 a.m. But after working at Simon and Associates for almost a year, and living a couple of blocks away for most of that time, Kelsey was spoiled, and now living a mile away seemed like a let-down.

"I don't want you to have to sit around for hours every night waiting for me," Kelsey said to Tyler as they walked to the elevator in the basement of their condo. Kelsey had remembered to drive the BMW back home. In the morning, after Jade dropped Kelsey off at the office, Jade would ride the bus or walk back to Belltown to pick up her motorcycle. Jade preferred having her motorcycle to driving a car downtown every morning, and she wasn't comfortable borrowing Tyler's car every morning to drop Kelsey off, despite the fact that Tyler wouldn't care.

"I like waiting for you," Tyler said.

"That's very sweet," Kelsey said, stroking his hand with her finger as he pushed the elevator button, "But you have other things to do."

"I want to make sure that we have dinner every night," Tyler said firmly. "And I don't want you coming home late by yourself."

Kelsey considered what Tyler was saying. If Tyler went home after dinner, Kelsey would have to be escorted home by a bodyguard — which meant that one would have to come downtown, wait for her, escort her home, and go back to Medina, or wherever the guard lived. It would be a hassle for the staff.

"I know," Kelsey said as they got on the elevator.

"Next week, I'll be back at work. We can see what my hours look like then," Tyler said, pressing the button to their floor.

"OK," Kelsey agreed. Maybe she was making too much of this. They had managed to work things out previously. Tyler stroked her side with his hand, and kissed her, hard.

"Let's think about something else," he said.

Kelsey smiled at him. "I can do that," she replied as she kissed him back.

Kelsey cuddled Tyler early on Saturday morning, and he kissed her. Kelsey had got through a relatively peaceful Friday, where she and Jake had spent two hours walking Tiana through a software licensing agreement, and Tyler had arrived at 8 p.m. with another dinner from Margaret. Now Kelsey just had to motivate herself to go back to work.

"Stay," Tyler said.

"You know I can't," Kelsey replied. As it was, she would be leaving Simon and Associates relatively early for a Saturday. Ryan and Jess had invited them to dinner, and before they went, the couple would give the Olsens a tour of their new house.

"Quit," Tyler said.

"No," Kelsey said. She looked at Tyler. "Stop pouting." Kelsey put her finger to Tyler's lips, and he kissed it. "I'll see you soon."

"I know. But I'll miss you," Tyler said.

"I'll miss you too," Kelsey said. She ran her hand through Tyler's hair, and he readjusted his hands behind her back. He kissed her bare collarbone.

"Are you sure you can't stay?" Tyler asked seductively.

Kelsey closed her eyes as she fell under his spell.

"Maybe for just a minute," she breathed.

Tyler and Kelsey drove across 520 at 5 p.m. in the silver Porsche. Kelsey had her window down, and her blonde hair streamed in the wind. She was humming along to one of her favorite summer songs.

Suddenly, a siren blared behind them, and Kelsey looked out of the back window at the flashing lights of a police car.

163

"You weren't speeding," Kelsey said as Tyler pulled over to the side of the road.

"I didn't think so," Tyler said. He put his hands on the top of the steering wheel, and a moment later the officer stepped into view.

"It's been a while..." the officer said, then he stopped speaking and looked surprised. "Who are you?" he asked Tyler.

"Tyler Olsen," Tyler said. Kelsey was confused. This wasn't a normal traffic stop.

"License and registration," the officer ordered.

Tyler pulled out both, and handed them to the officer.

"Wait here," the officer said, stepping away from the car.

"I know what happened," Tyler said, leaning back in the driver's seat.

"What's going on?" Kelsey said, puzzled.

"He recognized Ryan's car," Tyler said.

"Oh," Kelsey said. She understood too. Ryan's Porsche had probably sped across this highway a thousand times.

The officer reappeared at the window. "Here you go," he said, returning Tyler's license and registration.

"Thank you," Tyler said. The officer walked back to his car and drove off. Tyler started the car, and pulled off the side of the road.

"I wonder how many times you're going to get stopped driving this car," Kelsey mused.

"I guess we're going to find out," Tyler said as they drove off the highway, taking the exit to Medina.

A few minutes later, Tyler drove into the compound gates, and turned right. Kelsey looked at the house in front of her in surprise. It was enormous, multiple times bigger than Kelsey had realized. Every time she had been at Lisa's since the purchase of the newest house, Kelsey had noticed that construction was going on next door. What Kelsey hadn't realized was that the construction wasn't on the main house.

"Here we are," Tyler said, turning into a gigantic curved driveway. "What do you think?"

Kelsey looked at the house with wide eyes. She was speechless.

Tyler pulled into one of the numerous parking spots outside of the house, and turned off the car engine. He looked at Kelsey with a smile.

"Kelsey?" he asked.

"I don't even know what to say," she said in disbelief. The house she was looking at was three, maybe five times the size of the house that Tyler had grown up in.

"It's big, isn't it?" Tyler mused.

"Big is a bit of an understatement," Kelsey said. "How could anyone live here?"

"I guess Ryan and Jess are about to find out," Tyler shrugged. He opened his door and got out. Kelsey sat in her seat for another moment, shook her head to clear it, and followed him. They walked to the front door, and Kelsey tried to take it all with her eyes. It was impossible. The house was huge.

"Bro!" Ryan said happily as he opened the front door. "Hey, Kels."

"Hi, Ryan," Kelsey said. Holding Tyler's hand, they walked into the entryway. Kelsey looked up at the ceiling. It was so high, she couldn't make out any details.

"Where's Jess?" Tyler asked as they followed Ryan across the intricate parquet floor.

"In the kitchen," Ryan said.

Kelsey looked everywhere, in awe. She wasn't sure that she had been in a building this large, never mind a house. Perhaps some of the buildings at Portland State rivaled this one, but she wasn't sure. She held Tyler's hand tightly as they walked behind Ryan to reach the kitchen. There was no way she wanted to get lost in this place.

"Jess," Ryan called out.

"Hi, Kelsey!" Jessica said excitedly. It took Kelsey a moment to spot Jess in the huge kitchen, but there she was, beaming. Kelsey let go of Tyler's hand and ran over to give Jessica a gentle hug.

"Hi, Jess," Kelsey said. She glanced around the space. The kitchen, which was bright, sunny and modern, was also about the size of her parents' entire house. "How are you feeling?" she asked.

"Good," Jessica said. "The twins are being kind. Saving up their bad behavior until they get out."

Kelsey smiled. "What did the doctor say?"

"She said we'll wait until the end of the month. If I'm not in labor by then, she'll induce."

"Let me find Mischa and Audrey," Ryan said, leaving the kitchen.

"The day nannies," Jess said. "They arrived on Tuesday."

"Oh, right. Happy birthday," Kelsey said. Tuesday had been Jess's birthday.

"Thanks," Jessica said.

"Did you have a good one?" Tyler asked.

"It was great," Jessica said. "I thought I would officially be a mommy by then, but the twins obviously have other ideas."

"They'll be here soon," Kelsey said.

"Thank goodness," Jessica said, as Ryan walked in, followed by two Taiwanese women, who looked about seventeen. They were both wearing t-shirts and jeans.

"This is Mischa and Audrey," Ryan said. Mischa had a bright stripe of blue hair mixed into the rest of her jet-black hair, while all of Audrey's hair was a pale pink.

"Hi," Kelsey and Tyler said.

"Hi," Mischa and Audrey replied.

"These are our friends Tyler and Kelsey," Jessica said. "They got married last weekend. Tyler is Lisa's son."

"Oh, Ms. Olsen. Next door," Mischa said.

"Lisa's been by here every day, checking to make sure that Jess is OK," Ryan said.

Kelsey glanced at Jess, who nodded. "She has. It's been really sweet," Jess said.

"Surprising," Tyler editorialized.

"Thanks," Ryan said to the women.

"It was nice to meet you," Audrey said, and she and Mischa left the room.

"Where are they from?" Tyler asked.

"Taipei," Jess said.

"Lisa says that Taiwanese have the best Mandarin accent," Ryan added.

"Are the twins learning Chinese?" Kelsey asked in surprise.

"Of course," Ryan said, as if it were obvious.

"Where are the other nannies?" Tyler asked.

"Others?" Kelsey asked.

"They aren't on site," Ryan replied nonchalantly. "You'll meet them later."

"How many nannies do you have?" Kelsey asked Jess.

"Four," Jess said, slowly standing up. Kelsey reached over to help her, but Jess waved her away. "I'm OK," she said, once she was upright. "Two for the day, and two for the night."

"Margaret said that a chef was coming too?" Tyler said. "I thought you were cooking," he said to Ryan.

"The chef is for the staff," Ryan said.

"So you have five new people," Kelsey said.

"Eight," Jess said. "The babies are each being assigned bodyguards and my *yuesao*, Vivi, will be here from Los Angeles next Friday."

"*Yuesao*?" Kelsey asked.

"She's like a mommy and baby advocate. Lisa heard about it from the Tactec staff in Taiwan, and she insisted that I have one for the first month. Her job is to make sure that I'm eating right, that the babies are happy, that sort of thing." Jess looked at the group. "We can start walking, so you can see the house."

"Are you sure you're OK?" Kelsey asked.

"I'm fine once I get moving. I'm just a little slow getting started." Jessica laughed. Ryan took Jessica's hand, and they began walking. Tyler put his arm around Kelsey's shoulders, and they followed.

"What do you want to see first?" Ryan asked.

"Anything," Tyler said. "How big is this house?"

"Twenty-five thousand square feet," Ryan replied. Kelsey looked at Tyler in disbelief. The house she had grown up in was less than two thousand square feet in size.

"How many bedrooms are there?" she managed to ask.

"Fifteen," Jess said.

"And you said Lisa's house was big," Tyler commented to Kelsey.

"We'll need the room for the babies," Ryan said unconcernedly.

"How many are you planning on having? Fifty?" Tyler said.

"We didn't pick this house, Tyler," Jessica reminded him.

"True," Tyler said, looking around.

"It's nice, though," Ryan said.

"Nice," Jess said looking back at Kelsey, who giggled.

The Olsens followed the Perkins couple around the main section of the first floor. There was an gigantic living room with a stunning view of Lake Washington. The living room was so large that it was broken up into three sections, and had two glass fireplaces. There was a huge interior family room, which still managed to be a little cozy. In addition to the twenty-seat screening room, there was a large conservatory, which was filled with a family-sized Parisian iron table, and a multitude of edible flowers and herbs, perfect for Ryan's cooking.

An enormous master bedroom sat overlooking the lake. There was a huge walk-in closet, which was empty, to Kelsey's surprise. There was also a large sitting room attached to the master bedroom, that seemed like the perfect place to sit and look at the lake on a quiet, rainy afternoon. The en-suite bathroom had a sauna, rain shower, and soaker tub, and reminded Kelsey of a deluxe spa.

In between these large spaces, there were a multitude of smaller ones. Pantries, walk-in linen closets, even a small telephone room. An art gallery corridor ran across the front of the house. It was filled with framed photographs and small drawings. Kelsey suspected that there was nothing particularly expensive displayed.

"And that's the first floor of the main house," Ryan said, as they paused at the bottom of the staircase.

"I think I need sustenance to see the rest of the house. I won't have the energy otherwise," Tyler joked.

Kelsey agreed. She couldn't believe that they had only seen one bedroom.

"Come along," Ryan said, walking up the stairs. "More to see."

"This is where we'll live," Jessica said as they reached the second floor. "There's four bedrooms up here, and a yoga room." They walked around. Each of the large bedrooms had a en-suite bath, just as elaborate as the one in the master bedroom downstairs, although a little smaller. Each one also had a walk-in closet, and Kelsey discovered the one where

Jessica's wardrobe was.

The nursery had two adorable cribs already, one with a blue sheet, the other with a pink gingham one. There were two rocking chairs, a large diaper-changing area, and even a baby scale.

The group walked into a large yoga studio. "Look at this, bro," Ryan said, turning on a light. A shimmering golden pink brick wall lit up.

"What is that?" Tyler asked, touching the wall.

"Himalayan salt," Ryan said.

"Why?" Tyler asked, as Kelsey touched the salt wall.

"It improves the air. Removes negative ions," Ryan shrugged.

"OK," Tyler said doubtfully.

"How come you decided to stay up here instead of taking the master bedroom?" Kelsey asked as they headed back down the staircase.

"There's just not going to be enough room downstairs with the kids. We figured we should have everyone upstairs. The master will make a nice guest room."

"Thanks for thinking of us," Tyler said to Jess.

"You're welcome anytime, bro," Ryan said. "So that's the main house. Should we go to the north or south wing first?"

"You live in a house with wings," Kelsey said to Jess, who she was now walking next to.

"Unbelievable," Jess said, shaking her head.

"Where does the staff live?" Tyler asked.

"South," Ryan replied. "It's closer to Lisa's."

"Let's see that," Tyler said.

They walked through a door, into the south wing.

"There are five bedrooms, seven baths, and a family room," Jess said as they walked through.

"Where is Security?" Tyler asked.

"They'll be in the annex," Ryan said.

"Where's that?" Kelsey asked.

"It's the building closest to Lisa's property line," Tyler explained. Kelsey realized that was the building that she had seen under construction.

"Security will be there, along with the chef and Jess's driver," Ryan said. "There are four bedrooms, a living room, and a kitchen."

"So the nannies live in this wing," Jessica said. They peeked into the one empty bedroom. Unlike the rest of the rooms that Kelsey had seen, which were decorated in a laid-back, welcoming Pacific Northwest style, this wing was more Asian-sophisticated, with warm whites and dark woods. Chinese artwork graced the wall, and a white orchid in a celadon pot sat on a dresser. Clearly this wing wasn't expecting to have any little Perkins children running around it.

The group left the south wing, back into the main house, and walked along the art corridor to the north wing.

"How many bedrooms are here?" Kelsey asked Jess.

"Originally it was the same as the South wing. Five bedrooms, seven baths. But it's a little different now," Jess said with a smile.

Kelsey understood why a moment later. Although the rooms were still there, three had all been repurposed. One had been turned into a giant playroom for children, already full of toys. A second was a giant playroom for adults, with a big-screen television, a bar, and a pool table. The third was a double office for Ryan and Jess to share, with a giant bookcase holding Ryan's cookbooks on the wall. The last two bedrooms remained, ready for guests. A long deck connected the rooms to the outside, and back to the main house.

"It's well-organized," Tyler commented. "I don't feel like I could be lost for days."

"Speak for yourself," Kelsey said. Tyler laughed.

"Let's show you outside," Ryan said. They walked back through the main house, and out to the deck off the living room.

"What a view," Kelsey breathed. It was stunning — Lake Washington was sparkling in all of its glory in front of them.

Ryan led them off the deck. A few steps away was an immense outdoor kitchen, with a large grill, a free-standing pizza oven, bar, picnic table, and seating area for at least 15. Within sight, Kelsey spotted something that made her smile.

"It's the ship from our wedding," she said, pointing.

"Lisa thought the kids might like it," Ryan said, "So they disassembled it and reassembled it here."

"Is there a swing?" Tyler asked.

"Two," Ryan said, puzzled.

"Just wondering," Tyler said, giving Kelsey a smile.

"Where's the pool?" Tyler asked, looking around the outdoor grounds. Kelsey spotted a tennis court in the distance.

"There isn't one," Ryan said, and from his tone, Kelsey could tell that he wasn't happy.

"Why?" Tyler asked.

"Bob and Lisa thought that it was too hazardous for the kids, so we have to go over to Lisa or Bob's to go swimming."

"They have a point," Tyler said.

"I guess. Lisa said we could build one when the kids were older."

"That's OK, then," Tyler said. "Do you have a gym?"

"We do. It has a spa and a sauna. It's in the basement," Ryan said. Tyler gave Kelsey an apologetic look. He knew that she was disappointed that their condo couldn't have one.

"This is a really nice house," Tyler commented.

"You sound surprised," Jess said.

"I guess I heard so many horror stories about the renovation from Jeffrey, that I was expecting to have to walk over bare wires and broken boards."

"That was last month, I think," Ryan said. "But Camille told the contractor that if it wasn't move-in ready by the 7th, he wouldn't be paid a dime. I think that motivated him." Kelsey didn't know Lisa's assistant, Camille, so she didn't know if Ryan was exaggerating. But whatever had happened before, the house was certainly ready now.

"There's a couple more things to do," Jess said. "Ryan would really like an outdoor meditation area near the water, and the boat landing needs some repair. But it's fine for now."

"It's really beautiful," Kelsey said.

"Thanks," Jessica said. "I hope that you guys will come visit us a lot."

Jessica paused. "And babysit," she added with a grin.

"Speaking of," Ryan said, "I signed you guys up for the newborn-care class for next Wednesday. Can you make it?"

Tyler glanced at Kelsey. "It's fine with me. Can you go, Kelsey?"

"That's OK," Kelsey said. This was the first time she had heard about the class, but if she was going to be babysitting, she knew it would be necessary.

"Great, it's from 6:30 to 10. You'll have the normal class until 9, then you'll have a infant CPR class afterward."

"OK," Tyler said.

"Lisa and Bob are going too," Ryan added.

Tyler gave him a look. "We have to take class with Lisa and Bob?"

"It will be fun," Ryan said.

"Is Bill Simon going?" Tyler asked.

"No," Ryan replied.

"Fine, then," Tyler said, as the group turned and walked back into the house. "So what are the grandparents going to be called?"

"Jess's mom wants to be Nana, just like she is with the other grandkids," Ryan said, as they stood in the living room. "Bob swears that he will answer to nothing but Bob, but Lisa wants to be called Lala."

"Lala?" Tyler said in amusement.

"Tyler, I think you might be surprised just how excited your mother is about the twins," Jessica commented.

"I guess that as long as she doesn't want to have any more of her own, it's fine," Tyler said. Kelsey thought about Tyler's statement. Although Lisa wasn't exactly prime childbearing age, with enough money and the right medical team it was certainly possible.

"She really wants to know the names we picked out," Ryan said.

"She'll find out soon enough," Jess commented. Kelsey had to admit she was curious as well. Ryan and Jess hadn't told anyone the names that they had picked out for the twins.

"Baby Quinoa," Tyler teased.

"Over my dead body," Jess said.

"Don't say that. There's nothing wrong with quinoa," Ryan said.

"I'm not naming my baby after a grain," Jessica said. "Someone else can name their children those hippy-trippy names."

"Too bad, Ryan," Tyler said. "But I'm sure that Lala will like whatever you pick out."

Hours later, Tyler and Kelsey sat in the car outside of the Perkins house, kissing. Kelsey looked into Tyler's eyes, which sparkled in the setting sun, and stroked his face with the palm of her hand. Once again she was wearing her engagement ring, which she had retrieved from Jess.

"Let's go," Tyler said, turning and starting the car. "I can't wait to be back home with you."

Kelsey put on her seatbelt and nodded. The feeling was mutual.

They headed toward the front gate, when they spotted a town car in front of them on the road. The town car abruptly stopped, and someone rolled down the back window.

"Tyler!" Lisa Olsen called out happily.

Tyler looked out his own open car window.

"Hi, Lisa," he said.

Lisa Olsen waved at him. "Come inside. Five minutes."

Tyler glanced at Kelsey. "OK?"

"It's fine," Kelsey agreed.

"OK," Tyler said to Lisa. The town car drove on, and Tyler turned to follow it. He parked, and he and Kelsey got out.

Lisa Olsen got out of her car too, but the person holding her door wasn't Martin, her driver. It was Bill Simon.

"What are you two doing here?" Lisa asked brightly, as she walked over to the couple. She was wearing coral-red capri pants and a coral twin-set to match. Kelsey thought she looked really cute. Lisa gave Tyler a kiss on the cheek.

"We came over to have dinner with Ryan and Jess," Tyler said. "They gave us a tour of the house."

"Did you like it?" Lisa asked as they began to walk towards the house.

"It's nice," Tyler said.

"Hi, Kelsey," Bill Simon said to her.

"Hi," Kelsey said. She felt very awkward, but of course she didn't have a reason to be. Bill gave her a smile, and Kelsey realized that he felt awkward as well. She supposed the only person who didn't feel strange about this meet-up was Lisa Olsen.

The group walked into Lisa's house, which now felt a little small to Kelsey. She knew that her opinion would return to normal in time, and Bill shut the door behind them.

Lisa whirled around, and her long brown hair brushed her shoulder.

"Bill, I need to talk to Tyler about next weekend. Can you give us a minute?" she said.

"Of course. Kelsey and I have some work to discuss," Bill said. Kelsey looked at Bill in surprise, but she followed him across the foyer to the kitchen, while Lisa and Tyler walked toward the family room.

"What's up?" Kelsey asked. She wasn't aware of any issues.

"What?" Bill asked her.

"With work?" Kelsey asked.

"Nothing," Bill said, distractedly. "Do you want some lemonade?"

"Um, sure," Kelsey said. Bill took down two glasses, and looked in the refrigerator. He pulled out a pitcher of lemonade and poured it into the glasses.

"Do we need sugar?" Kelsey asked. Bill looked at her, then laughed.

"Margaret now keeps two pitchers in the fridge. One with no sugar for Lisa, and one with sugar for me," Bill explained.

"OK," Kelsey said, taking a sip. It was refreshing.

"How was your visit to Ryan's house?" he asked.

"It's really big," Kelsey said.

Bill laughed. "It's a monster," he commented, taking a sip of his drink. "Ryan and Jess seem to be getting used to it, though."

Kelsey was a little surprised. She didn't realize that Bill Simon knew Ryan and Jess well enough to comment on their feelings. Kelsey supposed that just because Tyler was avoiding his mother and Bill, didn't mean that Ryan and Jess were. In fact, for all Kelsey knew, Ryan was in favor of Bill's relationship with Lisa.

"And of course, I think Bob's really happy to have them so close," Bill added.

Kelsey nodded. That was probably true. She knew that, despite the fact that they weren't living in the city any more, Jess was pleased that Bob was so close by. Family was very important to Jess, and Bob and Ryan were her family now.

"Ryan said that Lisa was very excited about the twins," Kelsey said. It was a little strange to talk to Bill like this, but Kelsey realized it was only because she hadn't recently. Despite the fact that Bill was her employer, Kelsey knew a lot about his personal life, and he about hers.

"Thrilled," Bill said. "Tyler should be happy. Lisa will be too busy playing with them to pressure the two of you into having kids."

Kelsey smiled. She knew from Erica that before the ink was dry on the marriage certificate, well-meaning relatives would start nagging about a couple's baby plans.

"Good," Kelsey said.

"Not ready for children yet, Kelsey?"

"No," she replied. "I need to focus on work."

"As your employer, I'm happy to hear that," Bill said, laughing. "Actually, that is something that I wanted to discuss with you, and since Lisa's taking forever, now's probably a good time."

"Yes?" Kelsey asked, taking another sip of her lemonade.

"I've hired five new associates, and I'm planning on putting all of them on M&A projects."

Kelsey wasn't happy to hear that. Even though the odds weren't great that a new associate would stay, it would have been nice for her and Jake to have some — even temporary — help.

"I'm willing to hear some arguments in favor of assigning one of them to IP," Bill continued. "But honestly, I think that you and Jake have things in control over there, but M&A really needs to have a lot of associates, because I've got quite a few new projects coming up this fall for the M&A team."

"It's fine," Kelsey said unwillingly.

"Great," Bill said, taking a sip of lemonade. "I knew I could depend on the two of you."

"Of course," Kelsey said. She wasn't looking forward to Jake's commentary when he found out that she hadn't made a case for them. Kelsey hoped that it didn't come up.

"Kelsey," Tyler said from behind her. Kelsey turned around. "Ready to go?"

Kelsey smiled at the sight of Tyler. "I'm ready," she said. She placed the glass on the table.

Tyler glanced at Bill Simon, then turned and walked out of the kitchen.

"Bye, Bill," Kelsey said. Bill didn't seem surprised at Tyler's lack of warmth, but Kelsey felt uncomfortable.

"See you on Monday," Bill said with a smile.

Kelsey left the kitchen and walked out to the foyer. Tyler stood there, arms crossed. He gave Kelsey a smile as she walked to him.

Tyler reached out and ran his hands down her arms.

"Sorry," he said.

"It's fine," Kelsey said. She took Tyler's hand and they left the house.

Tyler was quiet as they drove out of the compound.

"What did Lisa want?" Kelsey asked.

"She just wanted to talk about the Tactec picnic next week."

"Anything special?"

"I don't have to wear a suit," Tyler said. "And she asked me to let you know that because Ryan and Jess won't be there, we're probably going to be a lot busier."

"That's fine," Kelsey said. She had noticed that Jeffrey had already put her dress for the event in the closet. Once again, she would be wearing flat sandals. It was a little odd, thinking about it, because this time last year, she and Tyler had both been taking the Washington State Bar, but Kelsey knew that the lessons she had learned during her previous times escorting Tyler would come back to her. She did make a mental note to pick up some extra-strong sunscreen during the week. Considering how much work she had, perhaps she would ask Jeffrey to drop some off. He wasn't likely to mind.

Tyler was quiet again as they drove out of Medina.

"Tyler?" Kelsey asked.

"Yes?"

"When are you going to talk about Bill Simon?" she asked.

"Is there something to talk about?" Tyler asked.

"It seems like there might be," Kelsey said.

"I don't think so," Tyler replied.

"Really?" Kelsey said doubtfully.

"Really," Tyler said firmly.

Kelsey was silent as she thought about her next move. Tyler was clearly not happy about Bill Simon being in his mother's life, and although there wasn't a lot that he could do about that fact, Kelsey did think that talking through his emotions might be a good idea. Lisa had been back with Bill for several months, and it looked like Bill might be around for the long haul. Kelsey thought that Tyler should face that fact, instead of ignoring it and being rude to Bill in the process.

"Have you spoken to Zach's mom?" Kelsey asked.

"About what?"

"About Lisa and Bill," Kelsey replied.

"No," Tyler said.

"Do you think that you should?"

"Should what? Talk to Keiko?"

"Yes."

"No. I don't think that I should," Tyler replied as they turned onto 520.

There was a surprising amount of traffic on the road, but Kelsey supposed that it was because people were heading over to Seattle for the evening.

"So you're just going to be angry with Bill?" Kelsey asked.

"I'm not angry with Bill," Tyler replied.

"No?"

"No," Tyler said, as traffic ground to a stop. He looked at Kelsey, who looked back at him questioningly. "Kelsey, I don't know how I feel," he admitted.

Kelsey felt a bit of relief, now that Tyler was talking.

"I feel like a hypocrite. I spent months convincing Lisa that who I was dating was none of her business, and now I'm critiquing her boyfriend," Tyler said as traffic inched forward. "The difference is that that Lisa didn't know you, but I know Bill."

"You know him professionally, not personally," Kelsey pointed out.

"I know, but Keiko Payne knows him personally, and she's on my side."

"Maybe for different reasons, though."

"Maybe," Tyler agreed. "I just don't know what to do."

"You don't have to do anything."

"I'm not OK with that. Bill Simon isn't like those jerks I didn't know. He's a jerk I know too well."

Kelsey felt like she finally understood the problem. She thought for a moment before she spoke.

"Have you spoken to Lisa? Told her your concerns, while still acknowledging that it's her decision?"

"No, because I'm still upset with her too. There's a part of me that feels like maybe they deserve each other."

Kelsey took a deep breath. Perhaps there was a lot more to this problem than met the eye. She hadn't thought that she was opening a can of worms by discussing Bill and Lisa.

"Maybe I should talk to Keiko," Tyler said. "There's the possibility that she won't discuss Lisa and Bill with me, but it's worth a shot."

"Have you spoken to her before?" Kelsey asked.

"Keiko? Not a lot. Actually, I'll probably just tell Zach to talk to her. Once I'm talking to him again."

"What do you mean?"

"Kimmy. That was not funny," Tyler said.

Kelsey laughed. "It was. You aren't really angry with Zach?"

"I'm angry with everyone," Tyler said. "Except you."

Kelsey smiled, and Tyler glanced at her.

"I could fix that," Kelsey teased.

"Don't," Tyler warned. "I need you."

Kelsey beamed. "I like to hear that," she said. Tyler reached over, and stroked her leg.

Kelsey woke up in Tyler's arms on Sunday morning. Sunlight flooded through the windows, illuminating the bedroom.

"Hey," Tyler said, kissing Kelsey's hair.

"Good morning," Kelsey said blissfully, turning towards him. As always, her heart fluttered at the scrumptiousness that was Tyler Olsen upon waking up. Sexily scruffy with gently-rumpled chestnut-brown hair, Tyler was irresistible. Kelsey kissed him on the lips.

"How did you sleep?" Tyler asked.

"Fine. Dreaming of you," Kelsey replied as Tyler stroked her bare back. Kelsey felt herself getting warm, despite the fact that the room was cool.

"Me, too," Tyler said. He looked into Kelsey's eyes. "What should we do today?" he asked, pulling Kelsey closer and kissing her.

"One guess," Kelsey replied happily.

A few hours later, Kelsey's legs were draped over Tyler's as they sat together on the sofa. Kelsey was reading a book on her Kindle about mentoring, while Tyler was scrolling through a document on his tablet. They had eaten the scones — that Ryan had sent back with them — for breakfast a while ago, and Kelsey was getting hungry. She put her Kindle to the side.

"Should I make lunch?" Kelsey asked.

Tyler glanced up at her. "You don't have to. There's food in the fridge from Margaret."

Kelsey looked at Tyler curiously. The only thing that they had brought back last night were Ryan's scones.

"There is?" Kelsey asked.

"Sure," Tyler said nonchalantly.

"But we didn't see Margaret yesterday. And you didn't take anything from Lisa's house," Kelsey said, puzzled.

"It was delivered while we were out," Tyler replied. Kelsey walked to the refrigerator and opened the door. She looked at the contents with wide eyes. Tyler was right — there were several containers of cooked food in the fridge, along with a pitcher of mint lemonade and a tossed salad. Kelsey glanced on the kitchen counter. A glass cookie jar, which had been empty yesterday, was now full of M&M cookies.

"That was really nice," Kelsey said. "But Margaret doesn't need to cook for us."

"She's happy to," Tyler replied, without looking up.

"I know, but she has other things to do."

"Not really," Tyler said.

"Tyler."

"What?" Tyler said, looking up at Kelsey. Kelsey frowned, just a little. Although it was nice that Margaret had cooked for them, it was Sunday, and a part of Kelsey wanted to have the opportunity to make a nice meal for her new husband.

"Nothing. Do you want me to heat something up for you?" she asked, resignedly.

A while later, Kelsey and Tyler were walking hand-in-hand along the Myrtle Edwards Park path. Lots of people were out on the path, walking dogs, biking, and just enjoying the summer sun.

"What were you working on this morning?" Kelsey asked Tyler, pushing her sunglasses up to her hair.

Tyler looked thoughtful before he spoke.

"I was reviewing my trust accounts," he replied. "I hadn't had time to do it before we left for Port Townsend."

"I see," Kelsey said, and she fell silent.

Tyler glanced at her and sighed. "This wasn't supposed to be a problem," he commented.

"It isn't," Kelsey replied.

"I feel like it is."

"Your feelings are wrong," Kelsey replied firmly.

"I see," Tyler said, mirroring Kelsey's earlier comment.

"What do you want me to say?" Kelsey said. "You know that I love you."

"I do," Tyler said.

"Give me time," Kelsey said.

"I will, once you know what you're dealing with," Tyler said.

"What do you mean?"

"I'll give you the space that you need after you've talked to my advisors," Tyler said. "Not before."

"I haven't had time."

"They'll come to you," Tyler replied.

"That's not necessary. I'll make an appointment."

"When?" Tyler pressed.

"Why is this so important to you?" Kelsey asked. But of course she knew.

"Because you're important to me. And this is a part of my life that I want to share with you," Tyler replied.

"I know. Next month."

"Next month?" Tyler asked.

"Tyler, the twins are coming. We have the Tactec picnic to go to, and the summer associates are here. Give me a break, OK?" Kelsey said in exasperation.

Tyler lifted her hand and kissed the back of it. "It's only money," he said soothingly.

Kelsey peered at him. "Stop saying that," she said grumpily. "If it was only money, you wouldn't care if I talked to your financial advisors or not."

"I guess," Tyler said. "Have you talked to Papa Jefferson?"

Kelsey frowned.

"Kels, that's a five-minute phone call."

"I've been busy," she said. "And Papa knows what to do better than I do."

"OK," Tyler said doubtfully. "I'll ask Jeffrey to make an appointment for you in August."

Kelsey nodded. "Can we stop talking about this now?" she asked.

"If you like," Tyler replied.

"I would," Kelsey said.

A gentle wind blew off the water, pushing some blonde strands of hair into Kelsey's eyes, She brushed them away with her free hand.

"What do you want to talk about?" Tyler asked.

"What do you know about mentorship?" Kelsey asked. "I want to help Tiana in the office, but I don't know exactly how to start."

"So you can win the bet?" Tyler teased.

"Because it's the right thing to do," Kelsey replied. "I feel like Bill's been a good mentor to me, but I'm not sure that I understand why I feel that way."

"It's an interesting question," Tyler said. "Lisa assigned the Chief Technical Officer of Tactec the job of watching over me, and she said it was because as my mother, she didn't think that she could mentor me properly. But I've never really mentored anyone, so I wasn't sure what she meant."

"Don't you think you were a mentor to the Law Review staff?" Kelsey asked curiously.

Tyler shook his head. "I was their supervisor. I had a vested interest in wanting them to do the work, but I wouldn't call it mentorship."

"I have a vested interest in helping Tiana," Kelsey pointed out.

"Not really. Sure, you'll benefit if she sticks around for the summer, but I think she'll be the one who gets the most out of the relationship."

"I guess," Kelsey said.

"I think that Bill was a pretty good mentor to you, because he has spent a lot of time helping you think about what you want from your career."

"You think?" Kelsey asked.

"He's given you a lot of opportunities as your employer, but I think that Bill really wants you to get something out of being in his office. I don't think he would be happy if you leave without having a direction."

"I suppose that's true. Jake said that you told him to talk to Bill about his work, and that's why he stayed."

"Jake's a nice guy, but he was in over his head."

"He's better now," Kelsey said.

"Thanks to you, I'm sure."

"I'm not Jake's mentor."

"No, but you do a lot of his work," Tyler replied.

Kelsey laughed. There was some truth to that statement.

"So what has Bill done for you?" Tyler asked.

Kelsey thought. "Well, he's spent a lot of time talking to me about the work that I like to do."

"OK."

"And he's pointed me into the direction of a lot of resources. Books and CLEs."

"He's done the same for Tori," Tyler said.

"And for you too."

"Some," Tyler said. "Bill knows I wasn't planning on continuing to practice as a lawyer, so he wasn't concerned about whether I liked the kind of work I was doing in the office."

"That's true."

"What else?"

"I don't know. I guess I feel like if I have a problem, or if something doesn't make sense to me, I can go ask him, and I won't feel stupid. Alex was like that too."

"Your other mentor," Tyler commented.

"He saw you marry me. Stop thinking about Alex," Kelsey said.

"I'll try," Tyler replied.

"Anyway, I think that's it," Kelsey said.

"Well, that's what you can do for Tiana. Find out what kind of work that she likes doing, point her to some resources, and be a resource yourself."

"That's it?" Kelsey said.

"You don't think so?"

"I don't know. I think I need to be more proactive if I want her to stay. There's going to be a lot of stress, and a lot of pressure to leave when the other summer associates do."

"True, Devin's not going to be mentoring anyone, and Tori's got too much work to think about it."

"Bill said that all of the full-time associates are going over to M&A in September."

"I bet they are," Tyler said.

"What do you mean?" Kelsey asked.

"Now that he's dating Lisa Olsen, Bill Simon's become the lawyer of choice for anyone who might have a technology company to spin off, and perhaps sell to his girlfriend's company."

"Tyler," Kelsey scolded.

"It's true. Ask Bill yourself," Tyler replied. "It's the perfect way to get on Tactec's radar. Everyone knows that Lisa is very hands-on when it comes to acquisitions."

Kelsey supposed that Tyler had a point.

"Are you feeling better about Bill and Lisa today?"

"Not really," Tyler admitted. Kelsey hugged Tyler's arm. "But I'm going to have to get used to it. Bill's not going anywhere."

Kelsey didn't say anything, but she agreed with Tyler. Bill Simon already seemed to be a fixture in Lisa's life, which wasn't surprising given their past.

"Should we turn around?" Tyler asked. The granary was up ahead of them, and the path started to get more industrial and a little less interesting.

"Sure," Kelsey said. They turned on the path and started to head back downtown.

"I want you to be happy," Tyler said thoughtfully.

"I am happy," Kelsey said in surprise.

"You say that you are, but... I don't know."

"Tyler, I'm happy with you. That doesn't mean that my life is perfect," Kelsey said.

"Mine is. Now that I'm married to you."

Kelsey smiled. "You're very romantic, Mr. Olsen. But I don't think so."

"Kelsey, I've accepted everything else that isn't perfect in my life and resolved myself to it. You were the missing piece, and now everything's fine."

"Have you accepted your parents?"

"I've accepted that they are insane," Tyler replied. Kelsey giggled and Tyler smiled at her.

"That sounds like acceptance," Kelsey teased.

"It's as good as it's going to get," Tyler said.

Kelsey packed her gym bag in the bedroom for the next day. Tyler watched her as he lay in bed.

"So are you working out tomorrow?" Kelsey asked.

"Maybe at lunch," Tyler replied. "We'll see. I've been going to a lot of meetings lately."

"When is Lisa going to give you an actual title?" Kelsey asked. Tyler was still a consultant for Tactec.

"No idea."

"Does that bother you?"

"Not having a title? Not really. Anyway, once I have a title, I probably won't get paid."

"What do you mean?" Kelsey asked curiously.

"Lisa's probably going to ask me to donate my salary to charity," Tyler replied. "I'm not expected to now."

"Oh," Kelsey said.

"It's half your money. How do you feel about that?" Tyler asked.

"It's fine," Kelsey said. "I haven't given you half of my paycheck. Do you want it?"

"No," Tyler laughed. Kelsey zipped up the gym bag and joined Tyler in the bed. Tyler wrapped his bare arms around her, and Kelsey put her leg on top of his blue-jean-covered one.

"Once I have a title, I'm going to start needing to go to a lot more events, so you should start thinking about whether you want to join me."

"Of course I want to go with you," Kelsey said.

But Tyler shook his head. "Not every night you don't," he replied. Kelsey thought for a moment. She supposed that Tyler had a point. She couldn't leave work early every night to escort Tyler to work functions.

"OK, we can set some rules. Maybe I'll go on Fridays and Saturdays and let you handle the ones during the week."

"That's OK with me."

"I'll miss you, though," Kelsey said.

Tyler hugged her tightly. "I'll miss you too. It's so wonderful being married to you."

"Is it?" Kelsey teased.

"Waking up next to you," Tyler said happily. "Spending time with you. It's magical."

Kelsey stroked Tyler's face. "For me too," she said softly.

Tyler leaned over and kissed her. "There's something else I like doing with you," he said seductively.

"Is there?" Kelsey said.

"Yes," Tyler replied. "Should we?"

"We definitely should," Kelsey replied. Tyler's hands reached behind Kelsey, and he deftly unsnapped her bra. He leaned down and kissed her collarbone. Kelsey felt her heart pound as Tyler slipped down the strap on her shoulder, and she closed her eyes.

The next morning, Kelsey drove herself and Jade across town in her BMW. She parked at work, then Jade escorted her to the gym. As Kelsey ran, she felt frustrated by the new system, necessitated by living in Belltown. Although Belltown wasn't far from work, because of the distance, Jade had to park at Kelsey's home, be driven to work, then return to Kelsey's to pick up her motorcycle. And of course, Kelsey now had to drive her car back and forth from work, which meant that she and Tyler had to drive home separately.

As Kelsey ran, she knew that she was being overly fussy. It was only a few minutes drive between home and work. But added to parking on both ends, and the inconvenience to Jade, plus the fact that for months everything had been a quick walk away from her apartment — suddenly living in Belltown had lost its charm.

When Kelsey arrived at work, she was greeted by Jake, who had a frown on his face.

"A summer associate left," he said, in greeting.

"Who?" Kelsey said.

"Naomi," Jake said. Naomi was a first-year, and Kelsey had assumed that she wouldn't last long. She had struck Kelsey as a little scatter-brained.

"Don't worry," Kelsey said. "I have a plan."

"I hope so," Jake said. "I don't want to lose ten bucks."

Kelsey giggled. "Don't worry," she repeated with a wink. She walked into her office. A stunning arrangement of pink flowers graced her desk. She smiled as she moved them onto the client table and lifted out the note. She opened the note, and read it in surprise. Then she frowned, and picked up her telephone.

"Welcome back," Alex Carsten said when he picked up.

"Thanks. And thanks for the flowers. But I'm not coming back to Collins Nicol," Kelsey replied.

"I've been assigned the task of convincing you," Alex said.

"Alex."

"I know. But hear me out," Alex said hurriedly.

Kelsey tossed her gym tote on the desk and leaned against it. "OK," she said unwillingly.

"The assignment didn't come from Mary. It's from Thomas," Alex said. Kelsey wasn't particularly surprised. The managing partner of the firm, Thomas Collins, had been furious when Tactec and the Olsen and Perkins families had pulled their work from the firm. "He thinks that this was all a big misunderstanding, and that Mary overstepped her bounds."

Kelsey frowned. "It wasn't a misunderstanding. It was quite deliberate," she replied, referring to her firing at the hands of Mary White.

"Kels."

"Alex, I don't know what to say to you," Kelsey admitted. "I think the world of you, but I'm not coming back to Collins Nicol. Even if I did, it wouldn't matter. Tyler would make sure that any Tactec work didn't return."

"Even if Mary was fired?" Alex asked Kelsey bluntly. Kelsey took in a deep breath. She wasn't expecting those words. Alex's question hung in the air for a moment, as Kelsey thought.

"No. Not even then," Kelsey finally replied. Despite everything, Kelsey wouldn't feel good about getting revenge on Mary White. Kelsey's time at Collins Nicol was in the past, and Kelsey wanted to look toward the future, not dwell in events of more than a year ago. "Does Thomas Collins really want Tactec's work that badly?" she asked.

Alex paused before answering. "I think he does," he replied.

Kelsey thought he did too. When she had worked at Collins Nicol, it was clear to her that the work that Tactec sent over was considered some of the most important work in the firm. Only senior associates were allowed to work on it, and Alex's reputation at the firm had taken a significant blow when Tactec hadn't awarded Collins Nicol a share of work — that Alex had been assigned to get — during Kelsey's second summer.

"Alex, I can't help you," Kelsey said firmly. "Collins Nicol brought this problem on themselves." And as she said it, Kelsey knew that it was true. She had been a third-year law student, caught in the decisions of senior people at Collins Nicol and Tactec. There was nothing that she could have done then, and there was nothing that she wanted to do now. If Collins Nicol had stood up for Kelsey in spite of Tactec's threats, they wouldn't be in this position now.

"Kelsey, I spoke to Thomas for an hour last Friday," Alex said briskly, as if Kelsey was about to bring the conversation to a close. "He says that he didn't approve your firing, that Mary did it herself."

Kelsey could believe that that was true. Kelsey was a lowly summer associate. It was quite possible that Mary White had decided to dispose of her without checking in with Thomas Collins. It was certainly within Mary's rights as a partner in the firm.

Alex went on, "Thomas has spoken to Lisa Olsen, who made it quite clear that she didn't order your dismissal. Everyone thinks that Mary here and Sydney over at Tactec went rogue."

Kelsey lifted an eyebrow in disbelief. She could believe that Thomas didn't know, but she still had her doubts about her mother-in-law. Those feelings, however, Kelsey would keep to herself.

"Thomas wants us to start over. Sydney has left Tactec legal, and he feels that if Mary leaves Collins Nicol, that will clear the air."

Kelsey realized something. "So if Mary leaves, you'll be promoted?" she asked pointedly. Although there were other IP partners at Collins Nicol, if Tactec was this important, the partner who was closest to the Olsen family would find himself in a great position.

Alex paused, just a little too long, and Kelsey realized that she had hit the mark.

"Maybe," Alex admitted.

"This is what I get for inviting you to the wedding," Kelsey groused. Alex had been the only person from Collins Nicol invited, despite the fact that Lisa had known Thomas Collins for decades.

"Kelsey, it's really important," Alex said.

"Maybe it is to you, and to Thomas, but it isn't to me," Kelsey said simply.

"It could be," Alex said. "Don't you want to be partner someday?"

"Not like this," Kelsey said. Associates worked for years to become partner, and Kelsey could hear Alex's unspoken suggestion that Kelsey wouldn't have to if she rejoined Collins Nicol loud and clear. "I want to earn being partner," she said.

"You would."

"It's not earning it by asking my new husband to forgive and forget," Kelsey said, shaking her head.

"Think about it, OK?" Alex said. "At least let me go back to Thomas and tell him that you're willing to consider talking to us again."

"I'm always willing to talk to you, Alex," she replied.

"Thanks, Kelsey," Alex said, and she could hear the relief in his voice.

She wasn't surprised. Alex wouldn't want to have to go back to Thomas and tell him that Kelsey Olsen had turned him down flat.

"You're welcome. How long until you call me again, and ask me the same question?"

"I'll try to give you at least three months," Alex said honestly.

Kelsey laughed. "Fair enough," she replied.

"Let's have lunch sometime," Alex said. "I'm assuming that you have permanent dinner plans now."

"I do," Kelsey said with a grin.

"OK, Kelsey, the next time I call, it won't be for a favor. I promise," Alex said.

"I'm glad to hear that," Kelsey said. "But it was still nice to talk to you."

"You too," Alex said. "We miss having you around," he added. And this time, Kelsey knew it wasn't the Tactec work that Alex was talking about.

"I miss you all too," Kelsey said honestly. She had enjoyed working at Collins Nicol, which is why it had been such a blow when it had been taken away from her. "Take care, Alex."

"See you soon, Kelsey," Alex said, and they disconnected.

A beautiful bouquet of roses arrived from Tyler at noon, and Kelsey placed Alex's bouquet at the reception desk. Tiana arrived at Kelsey's office promptly at 2 p.m., as Kelsey had requested. To Kelsey's dismay, the second-year summer associate looked completely stressed out. But, as Kelsey had told Jake, over the weekend she had come up with a plan.

"How are things going?" Kelsey asked brightly, although she was pretty sure that she knew the answer.

Tiana looked glum. "Bill gave me this contract, and I have no idea how to start," she said.

"May I see it?" Kelsey asked.

Tiana looked surprised. "Sure, it's on the network," she said. "Cooper Watersmith is the client."

Kelsey typed the name of the client into her computer, and pulled up the contract in the firm's shared documents. She scanned it quickly. It was a standard licensing contract, but as always, Bill had added a bunch of comments that would probably make little sense to a second-year law student.

Kelsey looked back up at Tiana. "Well, the reason I asked you here is because I think it might be helpful if you and I and Jake met every couple of days and reviewed whatever projects that you're having problems with. Sometimes intellectual property terms can be difficult to sort out, and I wanted to make sure that you aren't feeling overwhelmed."

Tiana looked at Kelsey in surprise. "You have time to help me?" she said in disbelief.

"I'm going to make time," Kelsey replied. "I think it would be great if you stayed for the entire summer," she added, making sure that she didn't offer any incentives for Tiana to stay, per the rules of the bet.

"Mrs. Olsen, that would be great," Tiana breathed.

"Kelsey is fine. Why don't we get Jake, and start working through your contract?" Kelsey said, standing up, her comfy slippers on her feet.

"OK," Tiana smiled happily.

Kelsey went to get Jake, while Tiana walked over to the second IP summer associate's office to find out if he wanted to join them. A moment later, the foursome was sitting at the large conference table outside of Kelsey's office.

"This is awesome," Dirk said. "I had no idea how to start."

"We'll plan on doing this at least a couple of times a week," Kelsey said. "We don't want the two of you to get lost. We're a team." She glanced at Jake, who was stifling a laugh. She looked at him harshly. "Aren't we, Jake?" she challenged him.

"Absolutely," Jake said with a grin.

Later that Monday evening, after Kelsey had managed to work on her own projects, she sat at her desk, poking at a bowl of pesto risotto. Tyler had called her an hour earlier, to let her know that he would be unable to join her for dinner. It was his first day back at Tactec after two weeks away, and as he had predicted, now that the wedding was over, he was swamped with work. He had been disappointed, as Kelsey was. As a sort of apology, he had arranged to have dinner delivered to Kelsey. But Kelsey found herself a little upset at the gesture. As always, the food had been made by Margaret, and was completely delicious, but since the couple had returned, every time Kelsey ate Margaret's food, she felt a twinge of guilt for not cooking for Tyler herself.

"Hey, beautiful," Tyler said as he walked up to Kelsey's office doorway on Wednesday evening.

"Tyler!" Kelsey said happily, jumping up to greet him. She leapt into his arms and gave him a kiss.

"Best greeting ever," Tyler said, stroking her hair and returning her kiss. "Are you ready to be a parent?"

Kelsey giggled. "No. But I think I'm ready to learn how to be one," she replied.

The couple's first stop was in Belltown, where Kelsey dropped her car in the parking lot at home. Afterward, Kelsey and Tyler discussed work on their ride over to the hospital — where they would have baby care classes, and where Jessica would be giving birth within the next couple of weeks. They also discussed a whiteboard in Tactec's legal department, which Tyler had seen during his day. There was a list of baby names for the Perkins' twins, as selected by the staff. Tyler had taken a photo of the list, which included the names 'Rainbow and Summer' from Ryan's yoga friends, and 'Harley and Dave", from the lawyer in charge of IP litigation.

As they walked through the hall of the administration building of the hospital, they spotted Lisa and Bob, who were standing casually outside of the classroom, chatting as Lisa's bodyguard stood watch. However, the rest of the students seemed less relaxed, and in various stages of shock, excitement, and surprise at the fact that they would be spending the evening with two of the country's billionaires. Kelsey wondered what they thought as she walked up with a third.

"Hi," Lisa said as they walked up.

"Ready to change diapers?" Bob asked. From his look, he was less than thrilled.

Tyler shrugged. "What's the big deal. You did it, right?"

"Bob changed exactly three diapers," Lisa said, laughing.

"Maybe two," Bob replied.

"Seriously?" Tyler said.

"It's gross," Bob commented.

"It's not a big deal," Lisa said to him.

"Then I'll call you and you can do it," Bob retorted. The classroom door opened, and a bright-eyed nurse looked out.

"We're ready for you," she said cheerfully.

The class entered the room, and everyone took seats at a group of tables which had been placed in a circle — including, to Kelsey's surprise, Lisa's bodyguard. She realized that he was taking the class as well. Kelsey had met Rohan very briefly at the wedding, although of course, she had seen him several times. He was a very tall, very big, quite intimidating man, with South Indian heritage.

Tyler's bodyguard, Conor, was serious when he was working, but he was friendly, and had a ready smile. Kelsey wondered if Rohan had ever smiled. His dark eyes surveyed the entire room, and from his demeanor, Kelsey knew that despite the fact that he would be diapering plastic babies with the rest of the class for the next two hours, Lisa Olsen was as safe with Rohan around as she would be if she were sitting in her own living room.

The class began slowly, with a presentation which even Kelsey found a little basic. She had realized, though, that the class that Ryan had enrolled them in was for relatives and friends of the baby, and of course a nineteen-year-old aunt-to-be wouldn't have the same knowledge as a parent. Kelsey noticed that Lisa was taking notes on her Tactec phone, which surprised her a bit. Perhaps Lisa had forgotten what to do since Tyler was a baby.

After the presentation, each person was given a plastic baby, along with a set of diapers and what Kelsey assumed was necessary equipment for the job. Bob sighed audibly, and Lisa giggled, as Rohan sat unmoving next to her. Kelsey glanced at Tyler, who seemed calm.

"This will be your baby for the evening," the nurse said brightly. "Feel free to give her or him a name."

Kelsey glanced down at the Asian baby doll on the table in front of her.

"I'm naming mine Scooter," Tyler said to her.

"Scooter?" Kelsey asked.

"I understand that's what babies do when they are on the changing table," Tyler replied. Kelsey laughed.

"Lala? What are you naming yours?" Tyler said to his mother, who was one seat away from him, between Bob and Rohan.

"Tyler," Lisa said without hesitation, giving Tyler a smile.

"Funny," Tyler said. "Do you really want to be called 'Lala'?" he asked her, as Bob frowned at the doll in front of himself.

"It's cute. And I'm tired of children calling me Lisa," she said pointedly.

"I call you Mom sometimes," Tyler said in his defense.

"Lala's fine," Lisa replied. "It will be easy for the twins to say."

"Lala and Bob," Tyler teased.

"When you're a grandparent, Mr. Olsen, you'll get your opportunity to choose," Bob replied.

"OK," said the nurse. She stood in the middle of the circle of tables, with her assistant. "We're going to start off easy. Step one, gently lift the baby."

Kelsey lifted the baby's ankles, but noticed that a few of her classmates were awkwardly attempting to lift the baby completely off the table and into their arms. Perhaps the class wasn't basic enough.

"No, no," the nurse said helpfully, "The baby needs to stay on the table for the diaper change. We just need to have access to the lower half."

Kelsey glanced at Tyler, who was holding the baby's ankles with one hand, and had a wipe in his other hand. Clearly he had studied ahead.

She looked back down at the plastic baby. It was going to be a long evening.

"That was fun," Lisa enthused as the group walked down the hall of the hospital.

"It wasn't," Bob groused.

"Of course it was. Now you know how to take care of your grandchildren," Lisa said.

"I hope it's knowledge that I never need," Bob said. "Do you want to get a drink?"

"Sure," Lisa said.

"Do you two want to join us?" Bob asked Tyler. Tyler glanced at Kelsey, who thought for a split second. Although there was nothing that she wanted to do more than go home with Tyler, Kelsey also knew that if she was serious about improving family harmony on the Olsen side of the family, sometimes she would have to make sacrifices. And tonight would be one of those nights.

"That would be great," Kelsey said, to Tyler's clear surprise.

"Let's not go far. It's a work night for the children," Lisa teased, with a smile to Tyler.

After a few minutes of discussion, they decided to meet at a hotel bar downtown. Lisa, Bob, and Rohan got into Bob's Bentley, which Steve was driving, and Tyler followed them in the Porsche.

"You're sure you don't want to go back home, Mrs. Olsen?" Tyler asked as they drove over the University Bridge.

"It's not every day that we get to spend time with your family," Kelsey replied.

"Kelsey, I work for Tactec."

"You know what I mean," Kelsey said.

"I do," Tyler replied.

"Do you mind?" Kelsey asked.

"No," Tyler said. "I don't have to get up early in the morning."

Kelsey knew this. She had been surprised to find out the time that Tyler was expected at work. Although the company officially opened at 9 a.m., virtually no one was actually in the office until 10 a.m. Despite this, people weren't generally expected to work late hours. Between the flex-time, working at home, and the generous vacation time that Tactec employees received, the company was a stark contrast to Simon and Associates.

"But you do, so we won't stay long," Tyler added.

"One drink," Kelsey said. "Then we can go home and go to bed."

Tyler glanced at her and Kelsey smiled seductively at him.

"This is going to be the fastest drink ever," Tyler said.

A few minutes later Kelsey and Tyler walked into a luxurious bar, with floor-to-ceiling windows overlooking the street outside. Lights sparkled in the darkness beyond the windows, as Tyler held out Kelsey's seat for her. Lisa and Bob were already seated at a table for four, and Rohan and Steve sat at the bar, talking quietly. As Tyler took his seat, a waiter came up to the table.

"May I take your order?" he asked.

"The bartender's favorite single malt Scotch whiskey, neat," Bob said.

"Lemon drop," said Lisa.

"Orange juice," Tyler replied.

"I'd like an Arnold Palmer," Kelsey said. On the drive down she had looked up 'non-alcoholic drinks at bar', and had found this one.

"Got any mixed nuts?" Bob asked, holding out the crystal bowl of salted peanuts that had been on the table.

"Of course, sir," the waiter said, taking the peanuts away and leaving to place their orders.

"Hard day?" Bob asked Lisa.

"Tiresome," Lisa replied, running her hand through her long, dark hair. "And I still need to wrap some things up when I get home."

Kelsey noticed that at least a couple of the dozen other patrons of the bar were glancing their way. She supposed that everyone around the table except her was used to being the center of attention.

"So, do you know the babies' names?" Bob asked Tyler as the waiter returned with a silver dish of mixed nuts. "Thanks," Bob said to the waiter.

"No idea," Tyler said.

"I told you he didn't know," Lisa said impatiently, reaching out and picking a cashew out of the dish with her manicured-but-bare nails.

"I was sure Ryan would have told you," Bob said, looking at Tyler.

Tyler shook his head no. "Ryan said that Jess said that it was bad luck to tell people before the babies were born," he replied.

"More wives' tales from the old country," Bob said, taking out a pistachio. "I grew up with that nonsense."

"We'll find out the names soon enough, Grampy," Lisa teased.

"I've warned you," Bob said sharply.

Lisa laughed. "There's no way that they are going to call you Bob," she said. "Jessica already said that she thinks it's disrespectful."

"I don't care. They asked me what I wanted to be called, and that's it. I don't need any more reminders that I'm getting old." Bob glanced at Tyler. "Having the boys married is bad enough."

"People age," Lisa said unconcernedly, taking another cashew.

"Not me. I'm fighting to the end," Bob replied.

"Good luck with that," Lisa said. "So what do you think that they're going to name them?" she asked Tyler.

"I have no idea," Tyler said. "You saw the board in Legal?" he asked.

Lisa laughed. "I did," she said.

"What board?" Bob asked. "What did it say?"

"Everyone's writing their favorite baby names down on a whiteboard outside Dev's office in Legal. You should see some of the names they've picked out," Lisa said.

"Indigo? Leaf? I swear if Ryan picks one of those granola names, I'm disinheriting him," Bob said as the waiter arrived with their drinks. Lisa's martini had a festive lemon curl balanced on the edge, while Kelsey's drink had a large lemon wedge on the side of the tall glass.

"Jessica won't let him," Tyler said confidently.

"I don't know. Jess doesn't seem to win a lot of battles with Ryan," Bob commented.

"She's too nice," Lisa said. "Don't be nice to Tyler, Kelsey. Get what you want."

Kelsey glanced up from her drink, surprised to hear that from her mother-in-law.

"You're supposed to be on my side," Tyler said.

"Forget it," Lisa said, taking a sip of her drink. "We women have to stick together."

"From what I hear, Kelsey can hold her own," Bob commented, picking up a walnut. Kelsey knew who Bob had heard that from, but remained silent.

Thanks, Morgan, she thought.

"Good," Lisa replied. She looked over at the waiter, who walked over to the table.

"May I borrow a pen?" she asked. The waiter handed her his. "Thank you," Lisa said charmingly, and the waiter returned to his station. Lisa took a cocktail napkin and began to write on it with the blue pen.

"What would you like the twins to be named, Bob?" she asked him.

"Anything as long as it's normal," Bob replied, taking a drink.

"Come on, play along," Lisa said.

Bob twirled the brown liquid in his glass thoughtfully.

"It would be nice if they named them after family," Bob said "But being that both sides changed their names after leaving Europe, I suppose there's no love lost for the names that they left behind. And I'm not sure that a kid named Bohdan is going to make it off the playground without being beaten up daily. Fine, put me down for Paul or Jason for a boy, Mary or Abigail for a girl."

"Very biblical," Tyler commented, taking a Brazil nut.

Bob shrugged. "I was raised in the Church."

"So was Jess. Maybe you'll get your wish," Lisa said, writing down the names. "How about you, Tyler?"

"I told Ryan that he should name one of them after me," Tyler replied.

"Tylerina?" Bob teased. Kelsey giggled.

"That's awful," Lisa said. "But the kind of thing Ryan would consider. How about you, Kelsey?"

Kelsey looked at Lisa in surprise once again.

"I really haven't thought about it," Kelsey admitted. Although the Perkins' twins names had been a parlor game for her and Tyler on long drives, she hadn't considered any names seriously.

"Really?" Lisa said. Kelsey shook her head. "We'll have to get you a baby name book when the time comes."

"How about you?" Tyler asked.

"Thomas, James, Joshua. I like British names," Lisa said.

"For a girl?" Bob asked.

"Olivia, Jane, Grace. Still British."

"That explains Tyler," Tyler said.

"Actually, when I was pregnant, I met a baby named Tyler." Lisa said, looking up from her list. "He was so cute and adorable, just like my baby was once he was born."

Tyler rolled his eyes.

Kelsey noticed that more people had started to look at their table in interest. For a split second she wondered why, then she realized. The ideas which had led to the birth of Tactec had been written on the back of a cocktail napkin, by these same two people. No wonder people were staring. They were probably imagining what brilliant, world-changing idea was being created on this paper napkin. Kelsey imagined that they would be quite surprised to find out what was really being discussed.

"How did you pick Ryan's name?" Kelsey asked Bob.

"It was Cherie's idea," Bob said. "I picked his middle name."

"Alexander the Great," Tyler commented.

Bob shrugged. "I like history," he said in reply.

"So is that how it works?" Tyler asked. "The mother picks the first name, the father gets the less important middle name."

"It's a small concession for sharing your body with another human being for nine months," Lisa commented.

"Why wasn't I Tyler Davis?" Tyler asked.

Lisa lifted an eyebrow. "You've asked me that before," she said.

"You've never answered," Tyler replied.

"Chris was out of the room when the birth certificate was filled out, probably," Bob said with a laugh.

"You were mine. Chris is lucky I put him down as the father," Lisa said unapologetically.

Kelsey was amused by Lisa's comment. It didn't matter whether Lisa wrote Chris's name or not. Everyone at the table knew that when a mother was married, the man that she was married to when she gave birth was legally presumed to be the father.

"I bet Bob didn't have that problem," Tyler said.

"No. I'm Ryan's father," Bob said, taking a sip of his drink. "By the way," he said, setting his glass down and looking severely at Lisa, "be nice to Cherie when she's here."

"I'm always nice to Cherie. The question is whether Cherie's going to be nice to me."

"Lisa, come on. You know what she thinks about us."

Kelsey could almost feel the tension of the secret that she, Tyler, and Lisa shared.

"She's wrong," Lisa said, sipping her drink.

"It's not Cherie's fault that she believed Chris. Do you expect her to be nice to the woman who stole her husband? Just be nice," Bob said.

Lisa shrugged. "I probably won't even see her for more than a minute. Have you talked to Ryan about her?"

"No, but I talked to Cherie and Jess. Cherie's going to stay at my house, and Ryan will probably avoid her when she goes to the hospital. She can visit the twins more when they're at home."

"What is Ryan's problem with her?" Lisa asked Tyler.

"I don't know," Tyler said. "He's never told me."

"It doesn't matter. Cherie and Jess get along fine, and Cherie will have a chance to see her grandchildren," Bob said.

"Seriously, you aren't even curious about why your son doesn't want to see his mother?" Lisa asked.

"Lisa, it's Ryan. Who knows what's going through his mind?" Bob said.

"I suppose you have a point," Lisa said. "But Tyler manages to deal with Chris." Tyler glanced at his mother, but said nothing. Did you talk to Chris at the wedding?" she asked Bob.

"The only time I saw Chris was when he was on stage, giving his speech," Bob said.

"Lucky you," Lisa said, giving Tyler a knowing look. Kelsey could imagine the words behind the look, being that Lisa had just given Christopher Davis 200 million dollars to keep the peace for her son.

"I'm sure you won't have to see him for a long time," Tyler said to her.

"Will it be a long time before you have children?" Lisa asked.

"Probably," Tyler replied.

"Fine. Then he can stay in New York until then," Lisa said.

"He's coming back to Seattle in the fall," Tyler said. "His sculpture is going to be unveiled."

"Don't invite me to dinner," Lisa said, taking a sip of her drink.

Tyler laughed. "I won't."

"I mean it, Tyler. You've spent all year ambushing me. Make sure you're done."

"I have what I want. I'll leave you alone," Tyler said. He smiled at Kelsey, as Lisa reached out and took a pistachio.

Kelsey thought that Lisa and Tyler's comments were interesting. It was true — Tyler had brought the proxy fight against Tactec, and had engineered a meeting between his warring parents, and both times Lisa had backed down and given Tyler what he wanted. Tyler had managed to clear out the Tactec board, marry Kelsey, and get a generous settlement for Chris. Kelsey supposed that Lisa Olsen had quite a few feelings about the actions of her only son.

"It's nice that the two of you have worked things out," Bob said in a pacifying voice.

Lisa laughed. "Robert Perkins. Always putting a lovely spin on things."

"That's my job, missy," Bob replied. "Anyway, it's worked out OK for you. The board's coming together, Chris can't sue you anymore, and you have a beautiful daughter-in-law."

"True," Lisa said.

"Tyler knows best," Tyler said.

"I don't think so," Lisa replied. "I think you got lucky this time."

Tyler winked at Kelsey, who blushed.

Lisa took another sip of her drink and set it on the polished wood table.

"Let's head back," she said.

Bob glanced at the waiter, who hurried over. "We'll take the check," he said, and the waiter walked off.

"What are you working on?" Tyler asked, as Kelsey finished her drink.

"Nothing interesting," Lisa replied. "There are just some problems I need to work out in Legal."

"When are you going to hire a replacement for Sydney?" Tyler asked. Lisa gave Tyler a dark look, as the waiter returned with the bill, which he placed on the table before leaving again.

"Don't remind me. Another problem you caused."

"Wasn't me," Tyler said coolly.

"Close enough," Lisa replied, crumpling her napkin. She stood and the others joined her. Bob pulled out his wallet, put down a one-hundred-dollar bill, and the group thanked Bob for paying. They all headed out of the bar, followed by Steve and Rohan.

As they left, Kelsey glanced over her shoulder. To her surprise, the waiter and two of the bar patrons were standing at their uncleared table, and one of them had his phone out. But Tyler gently steered Kelsey around the corner, and she lost sight of the bar.

"Are you ready for Saturday?" Lisa asked.

"I guess. But isn't it supposed to rain?" Tyler asked. Kelsey looked at him in surprise. It almost never rained in the summer in Seattle. Usually the weather was gorgeous and sunny.

"Global warming," Lisa commented.

"We have a rain plan," Bob said. "Postpone it a week. But of course the twins are due to show up then."

"Next time you'll have to tell Jessica not to have her due date coincide with the Chief Operating Officer's plans," Lisa teased.

"Ms. Olsen, the company picnic costs Tactec millions of dollars," Bob replied.

Lisa shrugged. "Don't go to see the twins at the hospital. You can see them after the picnic. Problem solved."

"And my CEO will miss the twins' birth too? So she can attend the picnic?" Bob said with a smile.

"Don't be ridiculous. I'm not missing my grandbabies," Lisa replied.

"You aren't even related to Ryan," Tyler said.

"Close enough," Lisa said.

Tyler and Kelsey said their goodbyes, then headed back home to Belltown. Kelsey changed into a cami and tap pants once they were back in the condo, then left the master bathroom and walked into the bedroom. Tyler smiled when she appeared, and stifled a big yawn.

Kelsey giggled. "We could go to sleep," she said to him.

"I'm not going anywhere with you in my bed," Tyler replied. He stretched out his arm and looked at Kelsey lovingly. Kelsey climbed into bed, and into his arms.

The next morning, Kelsey woke up to the quiet. Sunbeams shone into the bedroom. She looked at her sleeping husband and stroked his face. Kelsey smiled. It was nice to wake up next to him. She reached out and picked up her phone. It was surprisingly sunny.

Kelsey realized why as she looked at her phone.

"Oh no," she whispered. It was 8:15 a.m.

Kelsey's first thought was of Jade, who had probably been sitting somewhere waiting for Kelsey. Kelsey immediately sent her a message, apologizing.

No worries, Jade replied. *I knew you were out late. Did you need me?*

No, thanks. I'll ride in with Tyler, Kelsey wrote.

See you tomorrow, Jade responded.

OK. See you. Kelsey signed off with Jade, but she had a second message to send.

Running late, Kelsey wrote to Millie.

You aren't the only one, Millie wrote back. *Take your time.*

Kelsey set her phone back on the bedside table. Millie had added a bitmoji of herself winking in secrecy, and without asking, Kelsey knew the hidden message that Millie wanted her to receive — Bill was late because he was with Lisa. Of course, the CEO of Tactec didn't need to be at work early either. Kelsey knew that she wouldn't be sharing Millie's news with Tyler. She turned back to him, and he stirred.

"Hey, beautiful," he said, opening his eyes.

"Good morning," Kelsey said, giving him a kiss.

"It's about to be," Tyler replied.

"Where were you?" Jake asked irritably, when Kelsey finally walked into the office at 10:15.

"Don't ask," Kelsey replied. Tyler, delighted that his bride was still in bed, had seduced Kelsey with his charms, and since Kelsey was late anyway, she had allowed herself to be seduced. Of course it meant that Tyler had been late to work too. "What's up?"

"The interns need help," Jake said.

"So help them," Kelsey said unconcernedly.

"Nope. It's a software license. That's your job," Jake replied.

"Don't be silly," Kelsey said, taking her mail from Millie and walking with Jake back to their offices.

"Have fun," Jake said to her. Kelsey gave him a look as he walked into his office, but she bypassed her own and popped her head into Tiana's.

"Good morning," Kelsey said brightly. "Jake said that you needed some help?"

"Kelsey!" Tiana said excitedly. "Thank goodness," she said in relief.

"Don't worry," Kelsey said soothingly. "I'm here."

After she left Tiana's office, Kelsey finally walked into her own. She glanced down at the message she had received from Jess while she had been talking to Tiana.

What's this? Jess had written, forwarding Kelsey a link.

Kelsey opened it and laughed. It was an Instagram post of Lisa's note from the previous night, with the expected hash tags, #Tactec #LisaOlsen, #BobPerkins, and one Kelsey had started to see quite recently, #TKOlsen. Additionally, there was a note from the poster: *Ms. Olsen left this behind at the bar tonight. Thoughts?*

There were lots of comments, but all of them could be grouped into three categories:

Wow! The new OS naming system?

Names of the Perkins babies.

Names for the new Athena personal computer assistant.

Kelsey went back to Jessica's message and typed,

Bob and Lisa were listing their favorite names for the babies. Bob likes biblical ones, Lisa British.

Jessica replied with a laughing emoji.

I guess they're going to be disappointed then. Thanks, Jess wrote.

How are you?

Fine. Grumpy. Tired. Ready. How was baby class with the grandparents?

It was good. I learned a lot.

So you're ready too?

Ready to watch your super nannies do all of the diapering work, while the babies and I take cute selfies, Kelsey wrote.

Same here, Jess replied. *Everyone is here now. Except of course, for the babies.*

Any day now, Kelsey said soothingly.

It can't come soon enough, Jessica replied.

Bill walked up to Kelsey's office at 11:30, a white cup from Starbucks in his hand.

"Got a minute?" he asked.

"Sure," Kelsey said. Bill walked in and closed the door behind him. He sat in a chair and took a sip of coffee.

"We have a new client, and I'm giving them to you," he said, placing his cup on the client table. "It's a startup. Their offices are in Pioneer Square. They would like you to drop by during lunch next week."

"That's great," Kelsey said.

"They're interesting guys," Bill said with a smile. "I think you'll like working with them."

"What's their product?" Kelsey asked.

Bill smiled wider. "I'll let them explain it," he said, as he stood up. "I'll have Millie schedule the lunch for a week from today."

"That's fine," Kelsey said. She was really curious about what the startup did.

"Oh, also, I'm probably going to shift everyone's offices before the new associates come. OK with you?"

"It's fine," Kelsey said. She liked her office, but it wasn't as though she had time to look at the view.

"I knew you wouldn't care," Bill said. He took another deep drink of coffee. "See you later," he said as he left.

"Bye, Bill," Kelsey said. She turned in her chair and looked out the window. Then she turned back around and got back to work.

"So you need to make sure that the governing law is in Washington State," Kelsey said to Dirk as he sat in her office at 7 p.m. Although Dirk was a first-year law student, Bill had given him a very complicated software license to review.

"OK," Dirk said, putting a note in the margin.

"Hi," Tyler said from the doorway.

"Hi," Kelsey said, standing up. "One second," she said to Dirk.

"You're Tyler Olsen," Dirk said.

Tyler smiled. "I am," he replied.

Dirk looked confused as Kelsey walked over to Tyler.

"How do you know Tyler Olsen?" he asked her.

"I'm married to him," Kelsey replied. "Hang on," she said, pulling Tyler out of her office.

"Summer associate?" Tyler asked.

"Yes," Kelsey said, giving Tyler a kiss on the lips. "You're earlier than I expected."

"I know. There's a reason for that," he said. "Ryan and Jess are coming over to Seattle for dinner, and they asked us to join them."

"Really?" Kelsey said, happily. With her work schedule, and the Tactec picnic, Kelsey had wondered if she would manage to see Jess before the babies arrived. "What time did they want us to meet them?"

"Ryan said anytime before 8 should be fine. They're going to the mall."

Kelsey looked at Tyler in surprise. Jess had been content to stick around her new home lately.

"OK," she said. "Let me finish up with Dirk, and I'll be ready."

Tyler nodded. "I'll be in Tori's office. She said that she had a question for me." Kelsey gave Tyler another kiss, and walked back into her office. Dirk looked at her in awe.

"You're really married to Tyler Olsen? Lisa Olsen's son?"

"Yep," Kelsey said. "OK, next you're going to need to take a look at this force majeure clause." As she looked at his face, she could tell that he wasn't listening.

"Dirk?" she said.

"Kelsey, he's worth over two billion dollars," Dirk said.

Kelsey smiled at him. "Maybe. But he's priceless to me. Do you want to finish working on this contract?" Dirk nodded yes, and Kelsey continued.

A half-hour later, Kelsey and Tyler were walking hand-in-hand through the large department store connected to the mall. Ryan had messaged them that he and Jess were in the baby department.

"Look," Kelsey said excitedly. There was a giant fish tank, with numerous tropical fish swimming inside. She and Tyler paused to look, and they were rewarded by a beautiful royal-blue-and-yellow fish swimming past.

"Hey, bro," Ryan said as he walked up next to them.

"Hey. Where's Jess?" Tyler asked.

"Sitting over there," Ryan said, gesturing across the department store floor. Kelsey looked over and Jessica waved happily. Taking Tyler's hand, she led them towards Jess.

"Why did you come all the way over here?" Tyler asked Ryan as they walked.

"Jess said she was tired of the malls on the Eastside," Ryan said.

"Kels!" Jessica said. Kelsey leaned down for a hug. "I'm so glad that you guys could join us."

"We wouldn't have missed it. But I'm surprised that you wanted to leave home," Kelsey said.

Jessica moved as if to stand, and both Ryan and Tyler rushed to help her. Jessica stood, and took a moment to steady herself. The size of the twins made it difficult for her to find her center of balance.

"I was driving Ryan crazy in the house," Jessica said. "I've been fussy all day, and I started cleaning the kitchen around 4 p.m.. I don't know what's wrong with me."

"You're pretty close to your due date," Kelsey said. "Maybe it's a sign that the babies are about to show up?"

Jessica shook her head no. "I've been feeling the need to clean for a month. Anyway, we're going to have to drag these babies out. There's no sign that they're leaving on their own."

"Mrs. Perkins?" said a saleswoman, carrying a large bag.

"I'll take it, Jess," Tyler said.

"Thanks, Tyler," Jessica said as the saleswoman handed the bag to Tyler. "Let's go eat."

Ryan took Jessica's hand, and Tyler took Kelsey's as they walked slowly through the department store, toward the skybridge that connected it to the mall.

"So how was the class?" Jessica asked them.

"It was interesting," Tyler said. "There's a lot to remember."

"See, Jess. I said that too, and Jess said it was easy," Ryan pouted.

"You'll see," Jessica said. "Once you have some practice, it will start coming naturally to you."

"I'm not sure how much practice I'm going to get with our huge staff," Ryan commented.

"We're keeping all of them, Ryan," Jessica warned.

"I know," Ryan said. Kelsey could hear the disappointment in his voice.

"You'll be happy that you did," Tyler said.

"What do you know about it?" Ryan challenged him.

"I know that after that class, I can't imagine trying to take care of one without help, much less two," Tyler replied.

"I guess," Ryan conceded. "I just don't want to miss their milestones."

"You'll be around. You aren't going back to work until next year, right?" Tyler asked.

"Not then if I can get away with it," Ryan said.

"Then you can stay home," Jessica commented. "I'm going to be like Lisa."

Tyler laughed as they crossed the skybridge. "So you'll be back at work next month?" he asked. "I'm not sure Lisa lasted a week at home."

"I'll stay home in August," Jessica said, "But maybe September."

"You aren't," Ryan pouted again.

"We'll see," Jessica replied. "It's not like I have to go back full-time. I just don't know how much longer I can sit around the house."

"It will be more interesting with the babies," Ryan said.

"Interesting," Tyler teased.

"Just wait. You and Kelsey will want kids right away too," Ryan said. Tyler looked at Kelsey doubtfully. Kelsey had to agree. Help or no help, after the baby class, Kelsey knew that she wasn't ready to be a mother yet.

They walked around to the elevators, as Jessica didn't want to try to balance herself on the escalators, and rode down to the first floor. They walked over to Jessica's favorite Italian restaurant in Seattle and were seated.

Jessica sat heavily in her chair, and pushed herself far back from the table, so she would have plenty of room. She took a deep breath.

"OK?" Kelsey asked in concern.

Jessica nodded. "I'm fine," she said.

"Having a baby is hard work," Tyler commented.

Jessica grinned. "Yeah, I've heard about you, Mr. Olsen," she said.

"What do you mean?"

"Lisa has a ton of pregnancy stories," Jessica said.

"Like what?" Kelsey asked, curiously.

"Like the time Tyler kicked Lisa straight through a movie. It was the last one she managed to see see in a theater for years."

"Really?" Tyler laughed.

"She also slept in a chair for her last six weeks because she couldn't get comfortable in bed," Ryan said.

"And of course, you were eight days late. They really did have to drag you out of Lisa," Jessica commented.

Kelsey looked at Tyler, amused. "You were annoying Lisa even before you were born," she commented. Tyler laughed.

"What do you mean?" Ryan asked curiously.

"Lisa was on my case last night for ruining her year," Tyler said.

"You kind of have, bro," Ryan said.

"I told her I was done," Tyler said.

"You won't be if she gets more serious with Simon," Ryan replied.

"Don't ruin my night," Tyler said, looking at the menu.

"Have you talked to her about him?" Ryan pressed.

"I'm not you, Ryan, meddling in everything my parents do," Tyler commented.

Ryan looked at Tyler with his bright blue eyes.

"Don't ruin my night either, Tyler," Ryan said.

"Ryan, nine people lost their jobs because of you," Tyler said. And at that moment, Kelsey realized Tyler was talking about Morgan.

Ryan shrugged. "I didn't fire them," he said in his defense.

"Why did you have to tell Bob that you knew what happened on the yacht?" Tyler said. "No one's going to tell us anything any more."

"What are you worried about? Margaret's not going to stop talking about Lisa," Ryan said.

"Maybe. But everyone's going to stop talking to Margaret," Tyler replied.

"Drop it," Ryan said. "Let's order," he said, signaling to the waitress.

After they placed their orders, Kelsey stirred her iced tea. She and Jess looked at each other, and Kelsey knew that just as she was, Jess was trying to come up with a neutral topic to discuss. Ryan and Tyler still seemed unhappy.

"So can you take a day off when the babies come?" Jessica asked Kelsey.

"I doubt it," Tyler commented. Jessica bit her lip. Of course, that had been exactly the wrong topic.

"I can," Kelsey said hurriedly. "It's already been approved."

"Great," Jessica said, reaching out and taking a soft breadstick. "So, Tyler," Jessica said, starting again, "Lisa said that Margaret wasn't your nanny, that you shared a nanny with Ryan."

"I don't know," Tyler said. "Margaret's just always been there."

"Margaret knows your grandmother well?" Jessica asked, "I noticed that they spent a lot of time together at the wedding."

"Margaret is the youngest sister of my grandmother's best friend," Tyler said. "When my parents were getting divorced, Mormor asked Margaret to come over from Norway."

"Really?" Kelsey asked. This was the first time she had heard about Margaret's past.

"Margaret had just broken up with her fiance. Everyone thought she could use a change of scenery."

"Knowing Margaret, she needed to get out of town quick," Ryan piped in. Tyler laughed, and Kelsey was happy that the atmosphere had shifted.

"Definitely a possibility," Tyler said.

"She didn't want to go back?" Jessica asked.

"Margaret likes her freedom here," Tyler said. "She said that if she had gone back to Trondheim, her family would have made her get married. Here, she can do whatever she wants."

"I'm glad she's still here," Jessica said. "She's been really helpful since we moved in."

"Margaret's great," Ryan agreed.

"I have to say, though," Jessica said, and she paused as if she was wondering if she was bringing up an off-limits topic, "She doesn't always seem to get along with Lisa. They're both very headstrong."

"It's a miracle Lisa hasn't fired her," Ryan agreed.

Tyler looked at Ryan curiously. "Lisa can't fire Margaret," he said.

"What do you mean?" Kelsey said.

"Ryan, I can't believe you didn't know this," Tyler said. "Supposedly, after Margaret had been in Seattle for a few months, she and Lisa got into an argument about me. I don't know what about. I think Lisa thought Margaret was letting me have too much candy or something. Anyway, Lisa did fire Margaret. So Margaret calls Mormor and tells her that Lisa fired her. And Mormor tells Margaret to go back to Lisa and tell Lisa that she can't fire Margaret."

"No," Jessica said in shock.

"So Margaret did just that. She told Lisa that she couldn't be fired, and she went back to work. I don't think Lisa's tried to fire her since."

"Who told you that?" Ryan asked.

"Margaret did. I really can't believe you didn't know."

Ryan shrugged. "I just figured that Margaret was in the same category as

Rohan."

"No, Lisa actually likes Rohan. She just tolerates Margaret."

"What's Rohan's story?" Kelsey asked. She was fascinated by this discussion of the workings of the Olsen household.

Tyler tore a breadstick into two pieces. "Lisa and Keiko went to Mauritius when I was eight. Keiko had decided that Lisa needed a vacation. They were on the beach one day and a tourist kept flirting with Lisa. He wouldn't take no for an answer, but just at the moment that Lisa thought she was going to have to leave the beach, Rohan walked up and got rid of the guy. Rohan hung around the beach the rest of the day, and Lisa asked him if he would show her and Keiko around the island. He agreed and that's how they met."

"How did he end up here then?" Jessica asked. Kelsey was curious too.

"Rohan's family owns a computer hardware company, but Rohan wanted nothing to do with the business. Sometime over the three weeks she was there, Lisa offered him a job, and he took it."

"How did he end up doing security if he has a computer background?" Kelsey asked.

"That is a mystery," Tyler said.

"What do you mean?" Jessica asked.

"According to Conor, Rohan is really quiet about what he was doing before he came to Seattle. Conor's theory is that Rohan worked on Diego Garcia."

"Doing what?" Kelsey asked. She knew that there was a military base on Diego Garcia, but nothing more.

"Rohan could tell you, but then he'd have to kill you," Ryan said.

"No," Jessica said. "Rohan?"

"Conor's not afraid of anyone, but he won't cross Rohan," Tyler said.

"You two are joking with us," Jessica said dismissively.

"It's probably better that you believe that," Tyler replied.

Kelsey bit into her breadstick. Maybe she didn't want to know about the Olsen household, after all.

"Fine. Why did they go to Mauritius for vacation?" Jessica asked, spreading butter on her breadstick.

"It was the farthest vacation place from Seattle. Keiko literally took Lisa to the other side of the world. It didn't matter. They have phones and the internet, so Lisa worked anyway." Tyler replied.

At that moment, the waitress delivered their appetizers. Jessica dove into the fried calamari.

"I can finally eat what I want," she commented to Kelsey.

"Until the babies come," Ryan said.

Jessica rolled her eyes. "I'm not promising anything," she said.

"Jess, you want them to grow up strong. They'll still be eating whatever you're eating," Ryan replied.

"Stop guilt-tripping me," Jessica said, but she said it with a smile.

"You'll do what's best for them," Ryan said confidently.

Tyler offered Kelsey a piece of bruschetta, and she ate it from his fingers.

Ryan smiled at the couple. "I see married life is good," Ryan commented.

"Married life is great," Tyler replied.

"Told you," Ryan said, grinning at Jess.

"I'm glad that you waited to go on a long honeymoon. I'd hate it if you weren't here to meet the twins," Jessica said to Kelsey.

"Me, too," Kelsey agreed.

"Tyler, I forgot to tell you," Ryan said excitedly. "I can go to Canada. My visa was finally approved."

"Perfect timing," Tyler said sarcastically.

Ryan shrugged unconcernedly. "I'm sure I can take Jess one weekend."

"No time soon," Jessica said. "I'm not going to be in a different country from my children."

"We can all go," Ryan said positively.

"Everyone won't fit in the condo," Jessica said.

"We can stay in Tyler's house," Ryan replied. "Did you like it, Kelsey?"

Kelsey tried to avoid Tyler's eyes, because she knew that a blush was coming on.

"It was nice," she said softly. Tyler smiled broadly.

"How many bedrooms is it?" Jessica asked.

"Six," Tyler answered. Kelsey hadn't realized that there were so many. She had only been in one.

"It's nice, Jess. Right on the beach," Ryan said.

"You've been?" Jessica asked.

Ryan nodded.

"It's not far from the restaurant that we went to, Jess," Kelsey added. Jessica looked at her, and Kelsey could see the concern in her eyes. The Vancouver that Kelsey had experienced with Jess had been a very different one than she had enjoyed with Tyler. "We had a lot of fun," Kelsey added.

"Good," Jessica said, taking another calamari. She shifted in her seat.

"You're OK?" Ryan asked.

Jessica nodded, but she was frowning slightly. She tapped her phone and opened an app. A stopwatch appeared, and she tapped the timer.

"Jess?" Ryan persisted.

"What?" Jessica asked, biting her calamari.

"What are you timing?" Ryan asked.

"My contractions," Jessica said.

Ryan's blue eyes widened. "What do you mean?" he asked.

"I think I'm in labor," Jessica said, reaching for a bruschetta.

"You're what?" Ryan asked. Kelsey and Tyler looked at each other.

"Calm down. We have some time," Jessica said.

"How do you know?" Ryan asked.

Jessica rolled her eyes. "Didn't you read any of the books I gave you?" she asked.

"Of course I did," Ryan said petulantly.

"If you did," Jessica said calmly, "then you would know that you can time your contractions, and that will tell you if you're in active labor."

"Active labor vs. what?" Tyler asked.

"Early labor," Jessica said.

"And you're in early labor?" Ryan asked.

"It looks like it," Jessica said unconcernedly.

"Don't you need to go to the hospital?" Tyler asked.

"Not yet," Jessica said peacefully.

"When?" Ryan asked.

"In a bit," Jessica said.

Kelsey glanced at Ryan and Tyler, who both looked like they were in shock. Kelsey didn't know a lot about pregnancy, but she knew Jessica did, so if Jess wasn't concerned, Kelsey didn't think that she needed to be.

"Jess, we can have dinner wrapped up and take it with us," Tyler commented.

"It's fine. I don't want to sit around the hospital for the next twenty hours. We'll go later."

"Jess," Ryan said. Kelsey could hear the nerves in his voice.

"Relax," Jessica said. She glanced at the phone, then looked at Ryan. "The hospital is ten minutes away."

"Suppose you have the babies on the way?" Ryan said.

"That happens in the movies," Jessica said dismissively.

"It happens in real life too, Jess," Tyler said.

"Let me enjoy my dinner," Jessica said firmly. She looked at Kelsey. "Boys," she commented.

Ryan and Tyler were completely still as Kelsey and Jessica continued to eat. Tyler surveyed Jessica.

"Should we tell Cherie and your mom?" Tyler asked.

Jessica shook her head. "It's too early."

"It takes six hours to fly across the country," Tyler said.

"I'll probably be in active labor that long," Jessica replied. "Kels, can you hand me the salt?"

Kelsey did so. Ryan looked at Jessica in disbelief.

"How can you be so calm?" he asked.

"Ryan, if I panic now, how do you think I'm going to react when the babies are here?" Jessica asked, as a waitress approached.

"Can I clear this for you?" she asked.

"Sure, thanks," Jessica said.

"Can you please bring out our dinners now?" Tyler asked.

"Of course," the waitress said before she left the table.

"Tyler, we haven't finished our appetizers," Jessica protested.

"We need to leave," Ryan said.

"We don't," Jessica replied.

Ryan fixed his blue eyes on his wife. "The second you're done, we're going straight to the hospital."

Jessica frowned and pushed the timer again. "There's no point. We can just go home."

"No way," Ryan said. "We're staying on this side of the lake."

"Fine. But I'm not sitting in the hospital all night," Jessica said.

"We'll stay at Tyler's," Ryan said firmly. "OK?"

"You don't mind?" Jessica asked doubtfully.

"Of course not. But are you sure you don't need to go to the hospital?" Tyler asked. He was clearly unconvinced.

"Don't worry. I won't have the babies in your living room," Jessica giggled.

Their dinners arrived quickly, but both Ryan and Tyler seemed to have lost their appetite. In the meantime, Jessica continued to time her contractions in between bites of tagliatelle.

"You should eat," Jessica said, pointing to Ryan's chicken.

"How can I eat?" Ryan asked her.

Jessica smiled. "Like this," she said, taking a bite of pasta.

"That does it," Ryan said, pulling out his phone. "I'm calling Lisa."

Jessica laughed. "That's not going to help you. She knows nothing about contractions. Lisa didn't even know she was in labor. They told her when she showed up for her doctor's appointment."

Ryan sighed and looked at Kelsey. "Kels," Ryan pleaded. "You're the biologist."

"Trust your wife," Kelsey said, taking a bite of ravioli. She chewed and swallowed, then said, "Jess knows more about babies and her body than any of us do."

"Thank you, Kelsey," Jessica said. "Can I have one?" she asked Kelsey, pointing at the ravioli with her fork.

"Of course," Kelsey said, pushing the plate toward Jessica. "Have as many as you want."

"What about the baby bag?" Ryan asked.

"You put it in the trunk, remember?" Jessica said.

"Right. OK," Ryan said. He frowned, and looked thoughtful, as if he were running through a list in his mind. Jessica, who looked completely unconcerned, took another bite of her pasta. She shifted again, and tapped the timer.

"Eat," Kelsey said to Tyler, pointing to his risotto.

Tyler glanced at Kelsey, startled. "OK," he said.

Jessica shook her head in amusement.

"So what happens next?" Ryan asked.

"We finish our dinner," Jessica said calmly.

"Then what?" Ryan demanded.

"Then we have dessert."

"Jess."

Jessica smiled. "Then we go to Tyler's house and relax. I'll keep timing my contractions, and when they are five minutes apart, you can drive me to the hospital."

"I'll drive you," Tyler said. "Ryan won't be in any state to do it."

"It might be late," Jessica said.

"It doesn't matter," Tyler said.

"OK. Thank you," Jessica said. She went back to eating.

"I think we should tell Bob," Ryan said.

"So he can stay up all night. No way," Jessica said. She frowned. "Then again, it's almost midnight on the east coast. Maybe we should call the mothers," she said thoughtfully.

Ryan picked up his phone.

"No," Jessica said firmly. We'll call them first thing in the morning. "I'll probably still be in labor."

"Jess," Ryan whined.

"Just eat," Jessica said impatiently.

"Fine," Ryan said, finally taking a bite of his dinner.

Kelsey turned to Tyler and stroked his face gently. She gave him a smile. Kelsey could tell that the usually-composed Tyler was well out of his comfort zone. It was one thing to diaper plastic babies in a classroom, but this was something completely different.

Ryan focused on finishing his food, while Jessica ate hers leisurely. Once she was done, she asked for the dessert menu.

Ryan looked pained. Jessica gave him a kiss.

"Plenty of time," she said. She squirmed again, and tapped the timer.

When dessert came, Kelsey gave Tyler a nudge and offered him a bite of her warm chocolate hazelnut cake with gelato. Neither Ryan nor Tyler had ordered dessert, perhaps in the hope that Jessica would agree to leave. However, Jessica had ordered both the warm chocolate hazelnut cake, plus an extra dish of gelato.

"This is great," Jessica said happily.

"You'll have to have it delivered when you're at home," Kelsey said.

Jessica shook her head. "Mom will be there. I'm sure she'll cook for me."

"I will too," Ryan said.

"Of course you will," Jessica said. "But I want you to spend lots of time with the babies."

Ryan nodded. He smiled for the first time in a while.

After Jessica finished her dessert, Tyler called the waitress over for the bill, and Ryan stood to help Jessica out of her seat.

"Are you sure that we can't go to the hospital?" Ryan asked hopefully.

"Later," Jessica said to him. "Are you sure that we can't go home, Ryan? I don't want to keep Tyler and Kelsey up."

"It's fine," Kelsey said. "We're not going to be able to sleep anyway."

"It's going to be a long time," Jessica said.

"You can't be sure," Ryan said.

"No, but I'm pretty confident," Jessica replied.

Tyler paid the bill, and reached in his pocket for his keys.

"Take Jessica to our house. I need to take Kelsey to pick up her car," he said.

"No, that's OK," Kelsey said. She looked at Tyler. "I won't go to work tomorrow."

"Right, of course," Tyler said distractedly. Kelsey stroked his arm lovingly. He seemed almost as unnerved as Ryan.

"It will be fine," Kelsey said to him.

"OK," Tyler said doubtfully.

They arrived at the Belltown condo a short time later. Jessica changed into lounge pants, a tank top, and a soft gray hoodie from the clothes that were in her hospital bag. Ryan, who was sure that they would be going to the hospital any second, remained in his jeans. As the Perkins couple sat in the comfy new family room, Kelsey brought in her wool blanket from Kalaloch and placed it on an ottoman near Jessica's fluffy-slippered feet. Kelsey sat down on a chair next to Jess.

"OK, Jess said, setting her phone on the coffee table. "I've alerted Melody that I'm in early labor."

"What did she say?" Ryan asked.

"She said to let her know when I was heading to the hospital."

"That's it?" Ryan said in outrage.

"That's all," Jessica said peacefully.

"She didn't think that you needed to go in now?" Ryan asked in disbelief.

"No."

Ryan sighed unhappily.

"Ryan, it's a process. Early labor, then active labor, then babies. My contractions are still too far apart for anyone to be worrying." Jessica looked at Ryan lovingly. "We'll hang out here, watch a couple of movies, and I'll walk around a little bit. In a few hours, we'll probably be ready to leave."

Ryan nodded.

"If you say so."

"I do," Jessica said.

"Jess, there are snacks in the fridge, and the guest room is next door if you want to lie down," Tyler said.

"Thanks, Tyler. I'll be fine," Jessica said.

"Is Melody going to call your mom?" Ryan asked.

Jessica shook her head. "Not yet. The pilots have been alerted and the planes are on standby, but according to the plan, the mothers won't be contacted until I'm on the way to the hospital."

"Suppose the babies don't follow the plan?" Ryan asked testily.

"Calm down," Jessica said. "Everything's happening just the way it's supposed to."

"Is there anything else you need?" Tyler asked in concern.

"No," Jess said as Ryan pulled Tyler's blue-and-white crocheted blanket over her lap. "I'm sure we can find anything if we need to. They didn't change a lot when you moved in, although it is really cute."

"We'll give you a tour later," Kelsey said, standing up and handing Jess an extra pillow.

"That would be great," Jessica said. "Oof."

"What?"

"Foot in the ribs," Jessica said. She waved her hand. "Stop fussing over me. Go to bed and get some sleep. I'll let you know when I need to go."

"I'm staying right here," Ryan said.

"Fine. I'm not going to argue with you. But Kelsey and Tyler need to get some sleep if they're coming with us later."

"Come on, Tyler," Kelsey said, pulling his hand.

"Good night," Jessica said as they left.

Kelsey pulled Tyler into the master bedroom and shut the door. She gave him a kiss, took out some clothes, then went into the master bathroom to get ready for bed. For the first night in their short marriage, Kelsey thought that Tyler might have other things on his mind besides her body — so instead of her usual lingerie, she put on a Portland State tank top and Vikings lounge pants. Worst case, she could run out of the house by throwing a jacket over what she was wearing.

Kelsey ran her hand through her hair, and walked back into the bedroom. Tyler was lying in bed, hands behind his head, looking at the ceiling.

"Are you OK?" Kelsey asked, lying in bed next to him. Tyler placed his arm around Kelsey's shoulders. He looked at her seriously with his brown eyes.

"Do you know how to deliver a baby?" he asked.

Kelsey looked at him for a moment, then burst out laughing. "Is that what you're worried about?" she asked.

Tyler nodded.

"Tyler, Jess is fine. We won't have to deliver the babies."

"Are you sure?"

"I'm sure," Kelsey said with confidence.

"Why is Jess so calm?" Tyler asked.

"Hormones?" Kelsey guessed. "She's about to be a mother to two children. I'm sure Mother Nature doesn't see the point in panicking her just yet."

"You're sure she's going to be OK?" Tyler asked Kelsey, searching her eyes with his own.

"Positive."

"OK," Tyler said. He slipped his arm out from under Kelsey and got out of bed.

"What are you doing?" Kelsey asked.

"If you're sure Jess is fine, I'm locking the door," Tyler said. He walked over to the door and locked it. He turned and gave Kelsey a sexy smile. "We'll open it once we're done," he said in answer to her questioning look.

"Mr. Olsen, I thought we were going to bed," Kelsey teased.

Tyler lay down next her. He kissed her on the lips.

"We are in bed," he said huskily. He slipped his hand under her shirt and stroked her back. Tyler leaned down and kissed Kelsey's neck, and as he did so Kelsey felt her heart begin to pound. As Tyler pulled her against himself, Kelsey had only one thought. She hoped that Jessica was right and the babies took their time tonight.

Because at this moment, no one was leaving this bedroom.

Kelsey stirred in bed. Her phone had buzzed loudly with a notification. She reached over to the nightstand and picked it up as Tyler slept soundly next to her.

4:45 a.m., Kelsey read.

Kelsey blinked to focus as the bright light of the phone shone into her sleepy eyes. It was a message from Jessica, with just two words.

It's time.

Want my unreleased 5000-word story
Introducing the Billionaire Boys Club
and other free gifts from time to time?

Then join my mailing list at

http://www.caramillerbooks.com/inner-circle/

Subscribe now and read it now!

You can also follow me on Twitter and Facebook

43814655R00144